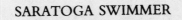

SARATOGA SWIMMER

Other titles in the
Allison & Busby American Crime Series:

STEPHEN DOBYNS

Saratoga Swimmer

Allison & Busby

LONDON

This edition first published in Great Britain by
Allison & Busby Ltd
6a Noel Street, London W1V 3RB

British Library Cataloguing in Publication Data:

Dobyns, Stephen
    Saratoga swimmer. – (Allison & Busby
    American crime).
    I. Title
    813'.54[F]   PS3554-02

    ISBN 0-85031-736-3
    ISBN 0-85031-737-1 Pbk

Printed in Great Britain by
Richard Clay Ltd, Bungay, Suffolk

FOR MY BROTHER

CHRISTOPHER DAY DOBYNS

1

IT WAS A cold evening for July, not quite 55°, and it
had been raining since noon, but the man climbing out of
the gray Mercedes parked in front of the Saratoga Springs
YMCA intended to go swimming. His name was Lew Ackerman and in his left hand he held a brown leather attaché
case, which contained a green Speedo suit, goggles, sham-
poo, and a large yellow bath towel.

Behind him, Ackerman's bodyguard and chauffeur, Jack
Krause, grabbed a copy of the *Racing Form* off the front
seat and locked the car doors. He didn't know how to
swim and found even baths suspect. In his twenty years
as a boxer, swimming had never been part of his physical
routine and now, despite his devotion to Ackerman, he
couldn't help but regret his employer's nightly visits to the
pool.

Ackerman passed through the double glass doors and
Krause hurried after him. The clock above the security
desk said 9:30. Ackerman checked it against his digital
watch and decided the clock was two minutes slow.

The young man at the desk glanced up. "Good evening,
Mr. Ackerman." He had been reading a magazine on jogging.

3

Ackerman slowed slightly. "How you doin, Bobby? How's the knee?"

"Better. I'm keeping it taped."

"That's the way." Ackerman turned right and passed through the door to the men's locker room with Krause behind him. In the game room to the left of the desk, two small boys who had paused to watch Ackerman walk through the lobby resumed their sword fight with broken pool cues.

Ackerman pulled off his tie and began unbuttoning his pale blue shirt as he passed through the locker room door. Removing the jacket of his tan three-piece suit, he handed it to Krause who shook it slightly and hung it in a locker. As Ackerman undressed, leaving his clothes on a bench, Krause folded the vest and shirt, gathered the shoes and socks and put them away.

Ackerman's body was well-tanned except for the white area at the hips normally covered by his bathing suit. As he pulled on the green suit, the white area disappeared. He was a tall, muscular man in his late forties, with wavy, blond hair and a square jaw. His nose had once been broken in a brawl and improperly reset so that it formed a vertical ripple in the middle of his face. In the fleshy part of his left arm above the elbow was the craterlike scar of an old bullet wound.

Ackerman went to the toilet, then returned tying the string of his suit. "That tomorrow's *Form?*" Ackerman nodded at the newspaper on the bench.

"Just came in."

"Red Fox is running at Belmont tomorrow. That'll be his last race before we bring him back up."

Krause picked up the paper and put it under his arm. "I've already put down my ten bucks," he said. "I just want to look over the competition."

4

Ackerman shook his head. "He's not ready. Just don't forget about him opening day, that's all. You sure you want to watch me swim? You know how you hate it."

Krause looked embarrassed. He was a heavyset man in his early fifties, nearly bald and with a round ragged face that seemed to bear a souvenir from each of his one hundred fights. He wore a dark brown suit and shiny black wing-tip shoes. "I don't mind," he said. "Anyway, you said I should keep an eye out."

"Go on. A night like this, it's warmer in here. Sit down and read your paper."

"Maybe I'll lift some weights," said Krause.

"Maybe you will." Ackerman walked to the shower room on the balls of his feet, turned on the water and remained under long enough to wet his hair, which he pushed back out of his face with one hand. Then he walked to the door of the pool on the far side of the showers. "See you later," he called.

The pool was twenty-five yards long and eight lanes wide. Ackerman entered by a door near the shallow end. To his right on the deck beyond the deep end sets of collapsible bleachers were pushed up against the wall. The air was thick and humid, smelling of chlorine. Sitting Indian-fashion on the diving board, the lifeguard, a high school girl in a blue tank suit, was reading a copy of *Cosmopolitan*.

Ackerman waved and walked toward her. "That's not going to help your swimming," he said.

The girl glanced up and smiled. "You take care of your stroke and I'll take care of mine. How many you going to do tonight?" Their voices echoed in the great empty space.

"Maybe I'll try a mile. I feel pretty good." Ackerman slapped his belly.

"Remember to keep your feet up."

Nodding, Ackerman spat into his goggles, then smeared

5

the saliva around with one finger until there was a squeaking noise. He walked to the edge of the pool, rinsed off the goggles, and began to put them on. Two other men were swimming and Ackerman knew them both: Philip Nathan, a blind swimmer, was slowly swimming laps in the far lane near where Ackerman had come in, while Jim Connor, a young man who tended bar and worked on a novel about racing, swam in the middle. As Connor approached the deep end of the pool, he waved at Ackerman without breaking stroke, did a flip turn and headed back the other way.

Ackerman chose a lane between Nathan and Connor. "Hey, Nathan," he called, "when're we going to race?"

"That you, Lew? Anytime, fella, anytime." Nathan's stroke was more of a slow dog paddle and he usually did one lap to four of Ackerman's or six of Connor's.

Ackerman put on his goggles, pushed his toes over the edge of the pool, and dove into the lane, keeping his head down so the goggles wouldn't be forced off. He had a long smooth stroke and he liked how the evenness of his stroke made his body feel like a machine. He arched his back slightly to keep his legs near the surface. Beneath him through the clear turquoise water was the black line he would follow back and forth. On either side of him he could occasionally see those parts of Nathan and Connor that were underwater: Nathan rough and angular, seeming to go against the water, Connor smooth and rhythmic like himself.

As the black line beneath him ended in a T, Ackerman dunked his head and swung up his legs in a flip turn. He didn't, however, blow enough air out through his nose and consequently took in water. He wrinkled his nose, trying to ignore the pain and maintain his smooth stroke, as he swam back toward the deep end. He was just learning the flip turn and still couldn't blow out properly.

6

For the next ten minutes, the swimmers continued without pause. The only noise was the sound of splashing, the whirr of the pumps circulating the water and the slight sound of the rain on the roof twenty-five feet above the pool. The whirr of the pumps, however, was loud enough to obscure other noises, and when the back door, marked Fire Exit, opened about six inches, the lifeguard, Judy Dunn, didn't look up from her magazine.

The fire exit door was at the bottom of five steps at the left hand corner of the shallow end of the pool. It let out on a narrow walkway between the south side of the YMCA and Sharri Tefila, the Jewish Community Center next door. The door was now open about a foot, letting in a cold draft of air. Because of the five steps, the shoulders of anyone outside were at the same level as the deck of the pool.

Philip Nathan stopped at the shallow end and stood up. He felt the draft from the open door, cocked his head, but didn't hear anything. He assumed someone was coming or going and thought no more of it. Then he began flicking both hands rapidly above the water, because he enjoyed the cool touch of the air on his wet skin.

When Nathan stood up, the door closed a few inches. Now it slowly opened again, although not wide enough for anyone to be seen. Ackerman was swimming toward the shallow end and had reached the middle of the pool. He had become comfortable with his stroke and was engaged in what he called violent meditation, making his mind go blank or simply remembering old poker hands. Connor was just negotiating another flip turn and was also swimming toward the shallow end.

When Ackerman was about twenty feet from the end, the fire exit door opened wide and a figure in a white raincoat and rain hat swiftly climbed the stairs and walked toward the edge of the pool. Disguising and mutilating his face under the white hat was a nylon stocking. As Ackerman approached the shallow end, the figure took a pistol from under his coat. Attached to the barrel was a long black tube. Sighting down the tube, the person fired. The bullet struck Ackerman in the middle of the back, catching him in mid-stroke with his left arm raised above his head and bringing him to a complete stop in the water. The next two bullets blew off the top of his head. The sound made by the pistol was no more than three loud puffing noises, which was heard by nobody but Nathan who lifted his head and stared blankly at the killer.

The first Jim Connor knew that anything was wrong was when the clear turquoise water turned pink, then red all around him: a great red cloud which grew thicker and thicker until he burst gasping from the water in time to see a person in a white raincoat and rain hat hurrying down the stairs to the fire exit. This hardly registered, however, as all his attention became fixed on Ackerman sinking below the surface a few feet away.

From her spot on the diving board, Judy Dunn could tell something awful had happened and she jumped to her feet. Seeing the far end of the pool slowly becoming red and Ackerman sinking into the water, she began to scream, dropping her magazine into the pool and pressing her fists to her face. She had not seen the person in the white raincoat or noticed the closing of the back door.

"What's wrong?" shouted Nathan. "Tell me what's wrong!"

The door to the locker room slammed open and Jack Krause came barreling through holding an upraised .38 revolver in his right hand.

2

PERHAPS THE terrible Harpe brothers as they swam out to plunder and slaughter the settlers drifting on flatboats down the Ohio River; perhaps any number of pirates, such as Captain George Wall who robbed and sank fishing boats off the Isles of Shoals after they had responded to his distress flag; or perhaps the Indians who swam out to kill Joshua Slocum as he rode at anchor for the night near the opening of the Strait of Magellan—perhaps these men had swum through blood. But Charlie Bradshaw thought it improbable. More likely it was the victims themselves who swam through blood, unfortunately their own, as they made their futile attempts at escape. True, Slocum's Indians, driven off by tacks spread on deck, must have swum back to shore with bloody feet, but the amount of blood must have been negligible.

Jim Connor stirred the ice cubes in his Vichy with one finger. "Does this mean you'll be out of a job?" he asked.

"It depends what Field does with the stable."

"What if they arrest Field?"

Charlie shook his head. "I can't believe he murdered Ackerman. He's not that kind of guy."

Charlie and Jim Connor sat in a corner booth at the Backstretch, a bar on the west side of Saratoga Springs. Ackerman had been murdered the previous Friday, and this Tuesday afternoon he had been buried in Green Ridge Cemetery. Charlie had gone to the funeral, partly because Ackerman was his friend, partly because he was Charlie's employer.

"It's common knowledge they weren't getting along," said Connor. "Even Peterson asked me if the guy in the raincoat could have been Field." Connor scratched the back of his head. Although only in his mid-twenties, his blond hair had begun to recede radically. When teased about it, he said it made him look like Lenin. It did, sort of. Connor wore a tight green alligator shirt which showed off his swimmer's shoulders. When he wasn't fiddling with his drink or his matches, he was picking at the alligator on his shirt.

"Could it have been Field?" asked Charlie.

He disapproved of Peterson giving Connor leading questions. Peterson was police chief of Saratoga Springs and had been Charlie's boss for ten of his twenty years on the force. However, two years ago, after returning to Saratoga after a mistaken adventure in New York City, Charlie had quit the police department. Most people assumed Charlie had been fired: an assumption Peterson never tried to contradict. Lew Ackerman, when he offered Charlie the job of head guard at Lorelei Stables, hadn't cared if Charlie had been fired or quit. He never asked about it. He knew Charlie would be first-rate and the rest didn't count.

"I couldn't see who it was," said Connor. "Maybe I saw a white blur. You know how it is. You don't really see anything in front of you." Connor's round, placid face seemed to tighten as the memory of Ackerman's death in the pool again took shape in his mind.

"You know, it didn't strike me until later," he continued, "I mean all that shit I was swimming through, the blood and brain tissue and, whatever it was, it didn't strike

10

me until later that that was Ackerman. I took a long shower at the pool, then at home, thinking about the whole thing, I took another, really scrubbed myself. I haven't gone back yet. You been there?"

"No. They drained the pool. It's supposed to open to-morrow." Charlie had been swimming regularly for the past year and now swam half a mile to a mile three days a week. Vaguely, he hoped that his improved physical condition would allow him to move through middle age with as much of his personal vanity intact as possible.

Charlie had meant to go to the pool the night Ackerman was killed, but it had been cold and rainy and Charlie hadn't felt like driving in from his small house on the lake. Since then, he had felt a little guilty, thinking he might have been able to do something had he been there. That was un-likely. But perhaps, he told himself, he might have seen the man in the white raincoat. Field was small and thin and would look so even in a heavy raincoat. Still, Charlie didn't believe Field would have murdered his partner, no matter how badly they were getting along.

"Were there a lot of hoods at the funeral?" asked Connor.

"I don't know. They didn't wear buttons."

"I liked Ackerman," said Connor, "but they say he knew a lot of crooks, you know, organized crime. He could have been killed for all sorts of reasons we'll never know about. Some mechanic could fly in here from the West Coast, waste Ackerman in the pool, and buzz back to L.A. the same night."

"Mechanic?"

"That's what they call them on TV. You know, hired killers."

Charlie nodded uncertainly. What Connor had said again made him question the theatrical nature of the murder. It was more like a murder on television than one in real life. He wondered if there was a reason for that. Then he gave it up and looked around for the waitress. The one he particularly wanted hadn't come in yet, so he ordered a beer from the bartender.

Despite the name of the Backstretch, the four walls of the long narrow room displayed eight-by-ten framed photographs of boxers. There must have been over a hundred and each bore a different inscription: "To Berney, a great guy, Jake LaMotta;" "To Berney, one in a million, Willie Pep." Berney McQuilkin was the owner of the Backstretch. Charlie had once studied these photographs with some care only to realize that the handwriting on each picture was the same. Tonight the bar was nearly empty. In the back room, which was a Chinese restaurant during the day and early evening, the topless dancer was lazily gyrating to "Sympathy for the Devil." In her right hand, she held a ham sandwich. Her audience consisted of a boy shooting pool and four poets from a nearby artists' colony who sat as close as possible to the miniature stage. At the bar, Berney McQuilkin was playing dollar poker with a wizened ex-jockey who had given up the track to become a TV repairman. The jockey's chin just reached the level of the bar, and whenever he won or lost he would slap the counter with a diminutive hand and shout, "Ha!"

"I heard Field didn't go to the funeral," said Connor.

Charlie nodded and drank some beer.

"Don't you consider that suspicious?"

"Maybe, I mean, perhaps he hated Ackerman, but that doesn't mean he shot him. Field didn't seem friendly with Lew, but then he isn't friendly with anyone. He's an accountant and he's got a lot of investments and he handles a lot of people's money, but he doesn't like people much.

12

He stays out at that house on the lake and all the paperwork gets brought to him." Charlie paused to think of Field alone in his big house and how little he knew about him. "Maybe I've spoken ten words to the man in two years," he continued. "He isn't particularly friendly, but he doesn't necessarily seem mean-hearted. He just seems blank."

"Weren't you surprised he wasn't at the funeral?"

"I didn't even realize it until later. It was huge. I mean, people came in from all over the country: a lot of big owners, rich people . . . ."

"And hoods . . . ."

"Sure, I guess there were hoods. Lew had all kinds of friends."

That morning, before the funeral, Charlie had thought it too bad that the day was clear and warm, one of the best days of the summer. He felt the weather should be bleak and the sky overcast to match his feelings. But then at the funeral someone had called it a fast track sort of day, and Charlie had realized that was what Ackerman would have preferred.

The service at the funeral home was so crowded that many people were forced to stand out on the porch. Nearly a hundred and fifty cars were in the procession to the cemetery. Charlie had recognized a congressman and a federal judge, numerous sports writers, besides the shadier mourners who interested Connor. There had also been people from every aspect of the racing world from the wealthiest owner to the guy that shoveled out the stalls: trainers, groups of jockeys, grooms, exercise boys, track officials, even some Pinkerton guards. And what struck Charlie was they all appeared to grieve. He wondered what Ackerman's three children had thought of it. They had flown in from San Francisco where they lived with their mother; they hadn't seen their father for several years. Even Chief Peterson had been there with about half the police department. Although he glowered at Charlie, he hadn't spoken.

At the cemetery a eulogy was delivered by Robert Dwyer, another stable owner in town who, like Ackerman, was part owner, part trainer, and part landlord for horses being trained away from the track or stabled temporarily. But while Ackerman had been still a relatively young man, Dwyer was silver headed and confined to a wheelchair, and it struck Charlie as ironic that the eulogy for someone so strong and healthy should be delivered by someone frail and infirm.

Dwyer had been pushed forward by his son-in-law, Wayne Curry, who stood behind the older man as Dwyer talked about Ackerman's service to the community and to racing: words which Charlie found overly conventional but which were made moving by the sounds and smells carried by an east wind from the stables surrounding Saratoga Raceway, the harness track, two blocks away.

"I heard Krause was pretty upset," said Connor. He had gotten some beer nuts from the bar and was ripping open the bag.

"I'd say that. For a moment it looked like he was going to jump down into the grave."

"Like in *Hamlet*." Connor offered some nuts to Charlie who shook his head.

"Maybe so. Personally, I don't think he was going to jump, but he ran to the edge when they lowered the coffin and he was crying. Somebody grabbed his arm." Charlie remembered the look on Krause's face as he stood at the side of the grave, staring down, as if all his wrinkles and badly healed boxing bruises had doubled in number, as if he were a man who now had nothing.

"I guess he feels pretty guilty," said Connor.

14

"How could he have known? There was no reason to think that Ackerman was going to get shot."

"It was his job," said Connor.

Charlie was going to argue this, when he saw the waitress, Doris Bailes, come into the bar. She was the only reason Charlie ever came to the Backstretch. Seeing Charlie and Connor, she walked over to their booth. Doris had short dark hair and an oval face so smooth and free from wrinkles that she looked more like 28 than the 38 she actually was. Even so, she was six years younger than Charlie and sometimes he worried that she rejected his advances because of his age, even though she had told him she wasn't going to get involved with anyone until divorce proceedings against her present husband were over and done with. She was a woman of medium height, slightly stocky and muscular in a way that Charlie found comforting. She wore Levi's, a blue blouse, and jogging shoes. Pinned to the blouse was a large white button with a picture of a whale.

Reaching Charlie, she touched his shoulder. "How was the funeral?"

"Five cars full of flowers and several hundred people. Everything Lew would have hated."

"Jack Bishop told me that the bodyguard tried to throw himself into the grave."

Bishop, a local realtor, hadn't even been there, to Charlie's recollection. "He just got too close to the edge and people got excited." Charlie considered for a moment, then turned to Connor. "What did Krause do that night at the pool. Did he go after the guy in the raincoat?"

Connor shook his head and swallowed a mouthful of nuts. "He came running in and when he saw Ackerman in the water, he didn't even pause. Jumped right in after him. Dumb guy couldn't even swim. He grabbed Ackerman, then began thrashing around. I had to drag him out." Connor

15

looked away and began rubbing his chin with his thumb. "Then he took a swing at me and went in again. He kept doing that until I had to drag Ackerman in too. It was a real mess. I mean, half of Ackerman's head was gone."

3

JUDGED BY ITSELF, the car parked along the road by Charlie's house meant nothing. But when he saw his house was dark as well, he kept on driving. The electric timer should have switched on the living room lamp at eight and shut it off at midnight. But now, at eleven o'clock, the house was dark and a strange car was parked on the road nearby.

Charlie drove another hundred yards and stopped. He had an old yellow Volkswagen Beetle and he pulled it onto the sand by the lake. Charlie had moved out to this small house, actually a cottage, on Saratoga Lake two years before when he left his wife and quit his job with the police department. What with well-meaning friends and his three interfering cousins, he wanted to be away from Saratoga during that change in his life. However, after friends and cousins alike heard he had been arrested in New York, had taken up with a girl young enough to be his daughter, and had been fired from his job with the Saratoga police department, they gave him all the privacy he could possibly want. He hadn't minded that privacy, but as he sat in his Volkswagen wondering what to do next he wished for a few people to call on. At last he took a deep breath and got out of the car.

Although Charlie had a pistol, it was tucked between some dish towels in a drawer in his kitchen; and although, what with swimming and general care, he was in better physical shape than at any other time of his life apart from basic training, the prospect of physical violence made him somewhat gloomy.

He was not a large man. Although stocky and even muscular, he was a good four inches under six feet. His round face was smooth and pink like a baby's, and he had large, blue, contemplative eyes that always seemed to be resting thoughtfully on something. His thinning hair was light brown and he brushed it straight back so people wouldn't think he was trying to hide his increasing baldness. He presented, he thought, an innocuous, anonymous figure, and he liked that. Other people would describe him as attentive, and Ackerman once told him he looked like a robin listening for a worm. That night Charlie had on a brown short-sleeve shirt and new khaki pants, and he was sorry at the prospect of a bit of roughhousing, as he called it, which would lead him to mess up his clothes.

It was a clear night and a three-quarter moon shone over the lake, making a silver moon path that shimmered across the water. Charlie's cottage was on Route 9p, a quarter of a mile past Snake Hill. While most of the cottages on the lake were packed together and nearly touched the pavement, Charlie had been able to buy one with a little space around it and set back from the road. It had originally been white, but Charlie had always disliked white houses and so the day after the closing he painted it dark blue with bright yellow trim around the windows and doors. Charlie had heard it said he bought the cottage with money made from various cocaine deals in New York City. Actually, the money came from savings and a five percent loan, which Ackerman had given him.

18

Charlie reached the strange car. It was a fairly new, maroon Oldsmobile with Saratoga plates. There was nothing inside except for a couple of white styrofoam cups and a pair of tan driving gloves. Taking a deep breath, Charlie moved on toward the driveway, keeping close to the bushes and tall maples that bordered the road.

Entering the driveway, he ducked down, trying to see through his windows thirty feet away. His cottage had a large living room with a fireplace, a bedroom, kitchen, and bathroom. The living room had windows on three sides and with the moon on the other side of the house, he hoped he could look through to see if anyone was waiting. Up until this moment, he still believed his house must be empty and kept chiding himself for being melodramatic. But then, as he got closer, he thought he saw someone, and as he moved to within fifteen feet of the house he made out the dark outline of a man standing in the middle of his living room. Charlie stepped back toward a big evergreen at the edge of his property. There were cicadas and he could hear frogs along the lake.

What Charlie wanted most was to tiptoe back to his car, drive to the nearest phone, and call the police. But as he thought of it he saw Chief Peterson's face as he had seen him that afternoon at the funeral: fat, rude, and diminishing. The face of someone who thought him a fool. A week ago Charlie might have called Ackerman or even now he might call one or more of the guards who worked for him at the stable. At this time of year, he had five men working under him. He could even go to the stable to borrow a gun. But as these alternatives flipped through his mind, he grew gloomier and gloomier, until at last he found himself ducking down and crossing the driveway toward his kitchen door. If he could open it quietly enough perhaps he could get to his pistol. He tried to remember if it was loaded. As he neared the woodpile, he picked up a thin, four-foot length of wood. A car passed on the road. From a cottage further down the lake, Charlie could hear laughter and rock 'n' roll music. He tried to think how many beers he had drunk at the Backstretch and wondered if he would be creeping toward his own house in the dark armed with a club if, like Connor, he had drunk only Saratoga Vichy.

Again, all his historical precedents were reversed. Although Charlie could name a hundred burglars and sneak thieves who had graduated from Marm Mandlebaum's burglar school at 79 Clinton Street in New York during the 1870s, he couldn't think of anyone, outside of a character in a P. G. Wodehouse novel, who had burgled his own house.

When Charlie reached his kitchen door, he opened the screen and tried the knob. It was unlocked. Gently, he turned the knob and pushed open the door. He was both surprised and pleased by how completely silent it was. He slipped through the door, shut the screen, then moved quietly across the tile floor of the kitchen, trying to remember loose floorboards and where the floor squeaked. The drawer with the gun was on the right side of the sink. As he slid it open, he began to think how simple it all was.

Then someone laid a hand on his shoulder. "What the fuck you pussyfooting through the back door for? You're lucky I'm not a nervous man."

Charlie gently pushed the drawer closed and tried to slow his breathing. It was Victor Plotz, another guard at the stable and someone Charlie thought of as his best friend.

"Was that you in the living room?" Charlie whispered.

"Nah, I was on the can."

"Then there's someone in the living room."

"Yeah, that's Krause. Whyn't you tell me you can't run the blender, the toaster, and the TV without bustin a fuse? Where do you keep'm anyway?"

20

"I ran out."

"Is that so. Whatcha carryin a cane for?"

Fifteen minutes later Charlie and Victor sat at the round dining room table watching Krause eat a huge plate of scrambled eggs by candlelight. It turned out that the body-guard had hardly eaten anything since Ackerman's death four days before. Krause was wearing a dark brown suit which looked rumpled and slept in. He kept putting down his fork and pushing back his chair as he argued with Charlie.

"I tell you, Ackerman left me ten grand. I'll let you have the whole thing."

"I still can't do it," said Charlie.

"That's a lotta moolah, Charlie," said Plotz. "Think of the good times."

"Keep out of this, Victor."

"Vic."

Charlie ignored him and drank some beer. Across the table Krause was staring at his eggs which seemed to flicker in the shadows thrown by the candles.

"You mean it's not enough?" asked Krause.

Charlie sighed. "It's not the money. It's just that there's no point. The police are investigating and even if they were doing nothing you still couldn't hire me. I mean, I'm nobody. I'm not a cop. I'm not a private detective. I've got no credentials. I'm a stable guard."

"Yeah, but you were a cop," said Krause. In the candle-light, Krause's round face appeared pock-marked and cratered like the surface of the moon. It was a sullen, unhappy face, and Charlie wished he could do something for it.

"Look, leave it to Peterson," said Charlie at last. "He's got to be working hard on this. A prominent citizen gunned down in the YMCA pool. It's as much as his job's worth to catch the guy."

Krause again pushed away his plate. "Peterson's nothing. He's looking in all the wrong places."

"How d'you mean?"

"He thinks either Lew was killed by Field or he was killed by hoods. Sure he knew a lotta hoods. Who don't? But that doesn't mean some hood killed him. Lew had a lotta friends. He was always on the up and up. Hoods don't shoot their buddies."

"What about Field?"

"What for? Maybe sometimes they quarreled, but Lew never spoke badly of him. No, there was something else on his mind."

Victor tapped Charlie's arm. "You listen to him, Charlie. I wouldn't of brought him over if I thought he was a screwball." Victor was drinking his beer in a large, 24-ounce stein with the name Munich written across it in black Germanic print and pictures of crenelated towers. He had brought it to Charlie's some weeks before so, as he said, he would have something decent to drink out of.

"So what was on his mind?" asked Charlie.

Krause had decided to eat some more eggs. After a moment, he delicately wiped his mouth on a bit of paper towel and resumed talking. "Something was bothering him. Most of the time I don't carry a gun. What's the point? Down in New York, maybe, but not in Saratoga. Anyway, two days before he's killed, he asks me if I'm carrying and I say no I'm not and he says maybe I'd better for a while."

"Did he seem frightened?" asked Charlie.

"No, I wouldn't say frightened. He seemed angry, like something had happened to make him angry."

Victor poked Charlie again. "See what I mean?"

"You have any idea what made him angry?"

"No, except it had been growing on him for about a week. Then, Tuesday night, he went off by himself after swimming. I asked him if he wanted me to drive him, but he said no, he wanted to go someplace on his own. So I told him to take the car, but he said he didn't need it."

"He went swimming at 9:30?"

"No, 7:30. He went at 9:30 Monday, Wednesday, and Friday, and he went at 7:30 on Tuesday and Thursday. So it was about 8:30 that I left him."

"Did he walk or was he picked up?"

"I don't know. Later, when he came in around 10:30, he said he'd gotten a ride back."

"You let him go even though he'd told you to start carrying a gun?" asked Victor.

"No, it was that night after he got back that he told me to start carrying it." Krause paused and glanced out the windows at the lake. One window was open and white curtains billowed slightly into the room.

Ackerman had lived in one of the Victorian mansions on North Broadway near the new Skidmore College campus. Krause lived there as well, while trainers, favorite jockeys, owners might stop in to stay as long as a month. All were looked after by an elderly Ukrainian woman who for years had kept a hotdog stand at the track until she retired to become Ackerman's housekeeper.

"And you have no idea where he went that night?" asked Charlie.

"None. He never said a word about it."

Charlie had seen Ackerman every day and they talked about horses or something to do with Charlie's job or just shot the breeze. For the week before Ackerman's death, Charlie had seen less of him, but that was because Charlie had been working nights. During spring and summer, when the stable was the busiest, Charlie had to hire three extra men, beginning in early April before the harness track opened. That's when he had offered Victor Plotz a job after

Victor had called to say he no longer wanted to live in New York City.

The last time Charlie saw Ackerman alive had been Friday afternoon. For the hundredth time Charlie wondered if Ackerman had seemed any different, but he'd seemed the same as ever: relaxed and comfortable with his world. Ackerman had told him what horses would be coming in that weekend, then teased him about his nonblooming romance with the waitress at the Backstretch. Thinking about it, Charlie could still see him standing at the rail of the training track, wearing his white Western shirt and jeans and with his sunglasses pushed up on his forehead, like he always did whenever he stopped to talk to somebody. As they had parted, they agreed to meet out at Lake Lonely at 6:30 Saturday evening, where they would rent a boat and fish for bass. They had done this several times before, and Saturday evening, even though he knew Ackerman was dead, Charlie made the mistake of keeping the date himself. Once out on the lake, he hadn't even bothered to bait his hook but just rowed around and felt miserable.

It seemed to Charlie that the fact Ackerman had said nothing to him about being more watchful suggested that if Ackerman was worried, his concern had little or nothing to do with the stable. Since Ackerman had few interests apart from horses, Charlie couldn't imagine what else might have bothered him.

"Did you tell Peterson about Ackerman going off?"

Krause turned back to Charlie and shrugged. "Yeah, but he didn't pay much attention to it. He figured Lew had a hot date. Sure Lew went out with a number of women, but he was never quiet about it. I'm not saying he bragged, but he liked women and, you know, he'd talk about it."

"Maybe some husband was after him," suggested Victor.

"I've had that happen myself and believe me it can be ticklish."

Charlie looked at his friend who was in his mid-fifties, nearly bald apart from the puffs of gray hair that rose from his scalp like dust kitties found under a bed, and had a nose big enough and red enough to light a ship safely to harbor. The fact that Victor had many girlfriends always gave Charlie hope about his own dim prospects.

"No," said Krause, "Lew made sure his girlfriends were unattached. I told that to Peterson and he just grinned. If he hadn't been a cop, well, he don't know shit from Shinola, that's why I think you could do a better job."

Charlie poured himself some more beer. "I'm not a cop and my reputation's so bad that nobody would talk to me even if I was."

"What if you just looked around a little bit? Ackerman thought you were pretty good, you know, the best. He was your friend too, right?" Krause mopped up the last of his eggs with a piece of bread. Even though he was overweight and now had food in his stomach, he still looked under-nourished somehow.

"Maybe," said Charlie, "I could talk to people at the stable." Even as he said it he knew he was committing himself to something he ought not to be doing. But sure Ackerman had been his friend, and if he had gone swimming that night maybe he could have done something.

"What if Charlie catches the guy?" asked Victor. "You tell him what you want when he does that. Listen to this, Charlie."

Krause put his hands together on the table in front of his plate. They were big hands and in the dim light with the fingers entwined they looked like a great pale chrysanthemum.

"I want you to let me kill him," Krause said.

25

4

RED FOX, a tall, two-year-old, chestnut colt, was being led along the shed rows toward the hot-walker by Petey Gomez when Charlie came around the corner of the barn and nearly bumped into them. Charlie was mostly suspicious of horses. More than once a horse had pushed its head out of its stall when he passed to make a grab for his guard's cap. But Red Fox was an exception. For a while, Ackerman had also been involved in breeding horses and still had a small interest in a farm in Kentucky. The colt had been born there shortly after Charlie started working for Ackerman, and Ackerman had given Charlie the honor of naming it.

Red Fox had been the name of Jesse James's horse during the three years after the terrible Northfield Raid when Jesse was laying low and running a small farm near Nashville. Going by the last name of Howard, Jesse had entered Red Fox in a number of Nashville races, riding him himself and winning several. Charlie couldn't imagine naming the horse anything else and Ackerman hadn't minded.

Charlie reached out and gently touched the horse's shoulder. Red Fox flicked his tail and shivered, the panniculus muscle quivering beneath the skin.

"Maybe he recognizes you," said Petey. He was a small, black-haired man who had been slightly too big and too

26

undisciplined an eater to be a jockey. He wore jeans, a ragged black T-shirt and a red Boston Red Sox cap. "You wanna wash him down?" he asked hopefully.

"Can't right now. When did he come in?"

"Brought him up from Belmont last night. Warner's got him scheduled to run opening day. Times were pretty good this morning."

Frank Warner was the trainer who worked with Ackerman. He was a few years older than Charlie, had been born and raised in Saratoga, and was a friend of Charlie's three older cousins. This, unfortunately, put him in the camp of those prominent citizens who thought of Charlie as shiftless. Although Warner had never seen Charlie behave in any way which could be considered shiftless, he was always careful to let Charlie know he had his eye on him and, what particularly irritated Charlie, to let it be known that if for some strange reason Charlie was not behaving irresponsibly at Lorelei Stables it was only because he, Frank Warner, was watching.

"You seen Frank this morning?" asked Charlie.

"Yeah, he's rushing around like he's got a tack up his ass. In fact, if he sees me standing here jawing, he'll probably bite my head off. Catch you later."

Gomez led Red Fox on toward the hot-walker, which already had three horses attached to its four horizontal arms. At the sight of the horses circling docilely between the training track and the row of stalls with their white paint and green trim shadowed by tall maples and oaks, Charlie felt nearly overcome with nostalgia and memories of forty Saratoga summers. And although the tourism and crowds often irritated him and, like the Chamber of Commerce, he often heard himself arguing that Saratoga was more than a one-month town, still, it was that one month he cared most about: four weeks of thoroughbred racing. Even as he thought about it Charlie could almost hear that noise which was a mixture of the sound of the sea and an approaching express train: the increasing roar as the horses circled the track, the swelling vocal crescendo as they reached the finish line, the mass shout of thirty thousand people which could be heard all over the east side of Saratoga. And Charlie, whether just walking along or directing traffic or trimming a hedge, would find himself lifting his head and holding his breath as if something immensely important were about to be settled in his life.

Now as opening day approached and more horses were being brought into town and the last bit of painting and cleaning and beautifying was being done to the race track, Charlie felt his body and mind quickening, his senses growing more alert. With this realization came a wave of anger that Ackerman wasn't here as well, that despite the time Ackerman spent at Belmont or at the Florida and California tracks, this coming month of August was the month he had liked best.

Charlie continued along the shed row toward Ackerman's office, past other horses, grooms, men and women rubbing down horses, a tack salesman, trainers, a jockey's agent. Most he knew and spoke to, and as he walked Charlie felt himself growing more and more angry at whoever had taken it upon himself to kill Ackerman and deny him this life. At the moment, the stables seemed subdued. No music or shouting or fooling around—everyone had a sense of Ackerman's absence, while beyond that was the question of what was going to happen next. Field might be arrested; Field might sell the stable; Field might hire a general manager who would run everything differently.

Ackerman's office was a small, white cottage with green trim about the same size as Charlie's cottage on the lake. It was located near the training track between two large white and green barns. One of the area's few remaining wine-glass elms stood nearby, planted, as Charlie knew, for the Centennial of 1876. Ackerman's office was locked and Charlie opened it with his passkey.

The room was musty and smelled of leather. Charlie opened a window that looked out on the track. The cottage consisted of one large room with fourteen windows looking out on all sides, making the room wonderfully bright but freezing in the winter. A red enamel Swedish wood stove stood on one side of the room, while across from it stood Ackerman's large Victorian desk. Charlie walked to the desk, sat down in the oak and red leather swivel chair, and looked around. On all four walls were photographs of every horse Ackerman had ever owned or trained. There was even a picture of Charlie standing next to Red Fox. Looking at it, Charlie remembered when Ackerman had taken it in early spring, how Ackerman had tried to convince Charlie to sit on the horse wearing a jockey's cap and how Charlie had refused, claiming it was beneath his dignity, not wanting Ackerman to know that he was a little afraid of horses.

The top of the desk was clean except for a black telephone with five lines, a Condition Book telling the eligibility re-quirements for the coming meet at Saratoga, and a gray metal box containing six-by-eight cards for all the horses that Ackerman owned or trained, showing where they were running, how well they were training, what their workout speeds had been and other pertinent information: taped legs, blinkers, doses of phenylbutazone and so on. Charlie glanced in the box, saw that it seemed to be in order and closed it.

The desk was covered with a new gray blotter. Ackerman was a compulsive doodler and usually went through four or five blotters a year. On this blotter was a telephone number, a drawing of a fire engine, a drawing of a horse, and the number 730. Charlie picked up the phone and dialed the telephone number only to discover it belonged to a pizza and sub shop in Saratoga.

Hanging up, Charlie opened the belly drawer. Along with pens in five colors, paper clips, and note pads, it contained a yellow plastic rose, a pair of swimming goggles and a snub-nosed .38. Charlie took out the rose, goggles, and revolver. Holding up the revolver, he saw it was empty. The goggles were resting on the blotter just over the number 730. They were Speedo goggles and rose tinted. Charlie was about to look through the other drawers when the door slammed open and Frank Warner stormed in.

"What're you doing in here?" he demanded.

The question took Charlie by surprise, because, thinking about it, he really didn't know what he was doing. He had told himself he wanted to look at Ackerman's office, but he didn't think he was looking for anything in particular, nor did he expect to find anything.

"I asked you a question, Bradshaw." Warner was about fifty and had the thin, wiry shape of a steeplechase jockey. He wore jeans and a red, yellow, and blue striped shirt.

Charlie leaned back in the chair. "Just thinking about Lew, I guess. Something upsetting you?" While Charlie didn't actually dislike Warner, he found him generally tiresome.

"Yeah, I got enough to do around here without checking up on your snooping." After storming into the office, Warner had stopped near the door. His glance kept shifting from Charlie to the gun on the gray blotter.

"I'm chief of security for Lorelei Stables and Lew was a friend of mine. I have a key to every building and every office, including your own. Why should I snoop? Come on, Frank, tell me what's on your mind."

Warner stayed where he was. He had a long, narrow face

like a garden spade. "Where'd that gun come from?" he asked.

"It was in the top drawer of the desk. It's empty. I didn't know Lew kept one around."

"Neither did I. Least it wasn't there two weeks ago."

Charlie restrained himself from asking Warner if he had been snooping. "How do you know?"

"I was looking for some stamps."

"What's upsetting you today?"

Warner's narrow shoulders sagged a little and he turned away. "I'm busy, that's all. Nobody knows what's going on. Field won't say anything. Meanwhile, more horses are arriving every day and I'm shorthanded."

"You mean because of Lew?"

"One of the grooms is sick, least his wife says he is."

"Who is it?"

"Neal Claremon."

"I don't recognize the name."

"He's a new guy. Lew hired him himself. Worked five days and now he's been sick five days. Not that I believe for two seconds that he's sick, mind you."

"Why not?"

"I keep calling and telling his wife to put him on the phone. She says he's too sick to talk on the phone. I figure a man too sick to talk on the phone should be in the hospital." As he spoke, Warner began cracking his fingers one by one, tugging at each finger like someone might pull at a ring he couldn't get off. "What I think is he's drinking, that's all. Also, the wife's a little rude. Now, if you're trying to protect your husband's job, you're not going to be rude to his boss."

"Have the police been talking to you?"

"Yeah, what of it?"

"You tell them about this Claremon?"

31

"No, why should they care if I got a groom who's a drunk? They were around here asking questions and interfering. Just like you're asking questions. Look, Bradshaw, I don't have the time . . . ."

"Just wait a second," said Charlie. "You have any ideas about why Lew might have been shot?"

Warner shoved his hands into his back pockets and began to look angry again. "Bradshaw, I train horses. Far as I could see Lew had nothing but friends. But he used to be a kinda wild guy. Who knows, maybe somebody he used to know just got out of jail. You got anything else to say?"

"When was this blotter replaced?"

"Jesus, Bradshaw . . . ."

"It's a serious question."

"A week, two weeks ago. Yeah, about two weeks ago."

"You had pizza around then? You were working late and Lew called out?"

"That's right, Sherlock. You going to solve this case for the cops? You and your team of stable guards? You'd better be careful or Field will hear you're being a nuisance and fire your ass. You have any more dumb questions? If not, I got work to do." Turning on his heel, Warner slammed out of the office as abruptly as he had entered.

Actually, Charlie had wanted to ask him about the number 730, but he shrugged it off. Then he quickly looked through the rest of the desk. There seemed nothing out of the ordinary. He looked again at the revolver and wondered why Ackerman had decided to keep it around. At last he put it back in the desk along with the goggles and yellow plastic rose. For several minutes, Charlie sat with his elbows on the desk and his chin in his hands, then he decided to walk over to his office on the other side of the stable.

As he walked back along the shed row, he saw Petey Gomez coming from the hot-walker with Red Fox.

Gomez called to him, "Hey, Charlie, whyn't you tell me you was going to find Lew's killer?"

"Who told you that?"

Petey pushed his Red Sox cap back on his head. "That guard, Plotz, he said you were going to teach the cops how to do it. Give 'em a few lessons in efficiency."

"Plotz has been pulling your leg."

"You mean you're not? Damn, Charlie, why not?"

Once as a policeman five years before Charlie had arrested Petey Gomez for passing a bad check. Petey had made the check out to himself and signed it John Whitney, of one of the big Saratoga racing families. It had been a check for $1,000 and Petey had tried to cash it in a small clothing store in payment for a three-piece suit of blue plush and a pair of red patent leather platform shoes. The store had called the police and Charlie had been sent over. On the way back to the station, Charlie had told Petey all the terrible things he would find in prison, how he wouldn't be able to protect himself, how he wouldn't be able to work for a stable again when he got out. Then, when they had nearly reached the police station, Charlie had let him go. Not only had Petey never again tried to pass a bad check, but he decided that Charlie was far smarter than any cop on television, presumably because he'd been smart enough to see through Petey's forgery.

"Because the cops can take care of it themselves," said Charlie.

Red Fox tried to rear up and Petey pulled him back down. "They couldn't find their way around the track," he said, patting the horse's neck.

"By the way," said Charlie, "did you get to know that new guy, Neal Claremon?"

"That guy that's out sick? I talked to him a little."

"What's he like?"

"I don't know, jumpy somehow. Like he expected a brick to fall on him."

"Ever see him with a bottle?"

"Never."

"Did he say anything about himself?"

"No, but he knew a lot about horses. Ackerman hired him instead of Warner and I saw him going into Ackerman's office a couple of times."

"Why'd Ackerman hire him?"

"Beats me. Guess he thought he needed another groom."

"What's he look like?"

"He's a real thin guy. You know the jockey Braulio Baeza? He's thin like Baeza was, but taller."

"Was anybody particularly friendly with Claremon?"

"Not that I could see. Stayed by himself a lot. I tried to talk to him a couple of times, but he'd just say yes or no or I dunno. Not much to build on. He wasn't rude or anything, just not too chummy."

Charlie left Gomez and headed toward Warner's office. He decided to get Claremon's address and go talk to him. If Claremon had been out the past five days, that meant the first day he had called in sick was the day after Ackerman had been murdered.

5

NEAL CLAREMON LIVED out on the north end of
Maple Avenue at the edge of Saratoga. As he drove across
Saratoga that Wednesday morning, Charlie was struck by
the increasing numbers of track people he saw downtown,
the number of horse trucks and milling tourists. If he had
still been with the police department, this was the week
when he would be receiving the names of pickpockets,
gamblers, confidence men, and common thugs which various
police departments around the country believed to be
heading toward Saratoga Springs.

Actually, Charlie's mother had lived on this part of Maple
Avenue before leaving Saratoga about a year before. His
mother had worked for the huge tourist hotels, the United
States and the Grand Union, during the thirties and forties;
had worked for the Grand Union until its final season in
1952, although during those last years work had been
spotty. Afterward, she had worked as a waitress until just
a year ago. That too had been seasonal, and as a child
Charlie and his mother moved several times a year, always
ending up with his prosperous and successful uncle, a
plumber, and his three sons who were still the bane of
Charlie's existence. When he was little, Charlie had
dreaded these moves which landed him each spring at his

35

uncle's house where his interests and accomplishments became decidedly second-rate and even questionable when compared to the successes of his cousins.

Despite this economically precarious existence, Hazel's ambition in life was to open a motel which would cater to the racing crowd: an ambition which had seemed pure fantasy until about a year ago when she had almost accidentally claimed a race horse which was turning out to be a winner.

Charlie stopped his Volkswagen across the street from Claremon's house, or rather the refinished garage that passed as a house. Charlie doubted it was any bigger than his own house, and although it had a second floor, it seemed no more than a small room made smaller by a sloping roof. Nearly touching the house was a slightly bigger but even more dilapidated two-story white house—the original possessor of the fixed-up garage which Claremon was presumably renting. In front of the house, a small dirty boy of about three on a rusty tricycle, wearing only a yellow T-shirt, was pursuing a spotted dog.

On one side of the house was a Gulf station and on the other was a motel called The Shady Nook. Charlie was surprised at that since Shady Nook was one of the names his mother had considered using for her own motel. The last time Charlie had been down this street, the motel had been called The Calvin Coolidge, and if Charlie hadn't received a postcard from his mother two days before, he would have suspected the motel of belonging to her. Since it didn't, she would be disappointed to scratch that name from her list of possibilities.

Hazel's card said only that Ever Ready was still winning and she urged him to make up his quarrel with his cousins because she would need their help when she returned to Saratoga. The card had come from Louisville, Kentucky.

As always Charlie was irritated with his mother's assumption that he had quarreled with his cousins, rather than admitting, as she well knew, that they had dropped him after his return from New York. In their minds, he was following in the footsteps of his hard-gambling, alcoholic father who had committed suicide when Charlie was four as a way of skipping out on $25,000 worth of IOU's. Actually, Charlie didn't mind being free from his cousins' everlasting advice. All that he minded about his current bad reputation was that he could no longer coach Little League baseball, which for Charlie, standing by third base on a warm summer evening and urging some little kid to slide, was what life was all about.

Charlie crossed the street to Claremon's house. As he reached the sidewalk, he noticed a white curtain with huge yellow flowers quiver slightly in a downstairs window. He was forced to redirect his attention immediately, however, by a high-pitched scream at knee level followed by a sharp pain in his left foot as the dirty boy in the dirty yellow T-shirt ran his tricycle into his leg.

"Gotcha," the boy said. He had bright red hair with a glob of what appeared to be tar stuck on top.

Charlie extricated himself from the tricycle and patted the boy on the shoulder. Then he continued toward Claremon's door. He knocked. There was no answer. He knocked again.

"You're an old fart," shouted the boy.

Charlie knocked a third time. Since he had seen the curtain move, he was prepared to knock all afternoon. He was just lifting his hand to knock again when the door opened and a small thin woman of about his age stood before him.

"What do you want?"

"I'd like to speak to Neal Claremon."

"He's sick."

"It's important."

"He's sleeping right now and I don't want to disturb him." The woman wore a blue checked gingham dress and stood with her arms crossed. Her bare elbows were so sharp and pointed that Charlie thought she could dig holes with them.

"I'm afraid I have to ask you to wake him up," said Charlie.

"Who are you anyway?"

"Chief of security, Lorelei Stables." Charlie straightened his back a little. Now that he was thinner, he hoped his bearing was somewhat more military. As a chubby policeman, he knew he had looked like a penguin in uniform.

The woman glanced down at her feet and shook her head. "I don't want to wake him up. Maybe you can try later or maybe I can help you in some way."

He found something familiar about her which he couldn't place. Perhaps he had seen her around Saratoga. She had large brown eyes and a sharp angular face that must have been quite pretty twenty years before. He tried to imagine it a little softer and less lined and again there was that nagging sense of familiarity.

"It has to do with his job at the stable and the death of his employer," said Charlie, lowering his voice a little. "If you don't let me see him, I'll go over to the motel, call the police, and wait until they arrive. I'm sorry to bother you, but I told you it was important."

The woman again looked down at her feet. "I was lying to you. He's not here." She looked ready to flinch, as if she had taken a lot of abuse in her life.

Charlie tried to speak gently. "Why should I believe you now?"

"Come in and see for yourself." She backed away from

the door and after a moment's hesitation Charlie followed her into a shabby living room with motel-modern furniture and cheap pine panelling on the walls.

"Where is he?" asked Charlie, glancing around.

"I've no idea." The woman walked back to the kitchen and Charlie followed. The kitchen was clean, white, and small with New England scenes from *Yankee* magazine thumbtacked above the sink.

In his mind, Charlie was sorting through his life year by year, trying to determine where he had known her. Turning away from a picture of a white steeple rising above a snow-covered village, Charlie saw the woman was climbing the stairs. He followed her up to the bedroom, but stood only in the doorway out of what he thought of as a rather stupid shyness, as if he thought this tired woman would seduce him or was afraid she might think he wanted to attack her. In any case, the bedroom was empty and the bed made and covered with a white chenille spread. Not only was Neal Claremon nowhere in evidence, but the room was so neat and tidy that it seemed completely unused. On the pine bureau were some cheaply framed photographs and looking at a wedding picture of a smiling young woman, who through disappointment and hard times had evolved into the woman standing in front of him, Charlie remembered where he had known her before. He was so taken back by this and felt such a wave of sympathy that he turned and descended the stairs. Mrs. Claremon followed him.

When he reached the bottom, he said, "I expect you do know where your husband is, and I'd appreciate it if you'd tell me. I don't mean to make trouble for him, but he might know something about Ackerman's murder and so I'd like to talk to him."

"I already told you, I don't know where he is." The woman went to the sink and tried to shut off a dripping faucet. Watching her, Charlie felt he was deceiving her by remembering who she was, while she, apparently, didn't recall him.

"If you don't tell me, then, as I say, I'll have to call the police and they'll ask you these questions."

The woman didn't answer but kept pushing at the handle of the dripping faucet. She had short gray hair and Charlie remembered when it had been brown and silky.

"Aren't you Janet Macomb?" he asked.

She turned quickly and stared at him, trying to place him, but not succeeding.

"I'm Charlie Bradshaw. Remember?"

She obviously didn't, although she still watched him intently. Charlie wondered if he had looked so different twenty-five years ago.

"We were in typing class together in high school," he said. "You were a year behind me. But I sat next to you, remember?"

This time Janet Macomb gave an abrupt laugh, then clapped her hand over her mouth, then folded her arms again. "We traded tests," she said at last.

Charlie nodded. "That's right."

Charlie had taken typing because his cousins had told him it would be useful in his future career. At that time they had planned for him to become a bookkeeper. Actually, it had been quite useful to him as a policeman since it speeded up the writing of endless reports. By some fluke Charlie had been an extremely fast and accurate typist, while Janet Macomb, who sat beside him, was the class dummy. Even when she managed forty words per minute, her endless mistakes often awarded her a minus score. Apart from typing class, Janet was successful and sought after: a cheer-leader who was also secretary in various school clubs.

They had been friendly and, although Charlie had never summoned up the courage to ask her out, he had once, before a major exam in the spring, offered to swap tests when it became clear that another low grade would lead to her flunking the class. She had agreed, and he had taken her sloppily typed page as his. Consequently, she had passed the course with a rockbottom C and Charlie's grade had dropped from an A to a B. After graduation and the army, he had never seen her again until now.

"Have you been in Saratoga all this time?" Charlie asked.

She shook her head. "We just came back about three years ago. I married Neal right out of high school. He'd been working at the track and was only up here for August. After we married, we moved down to Long Island. Neal had a job as a groom for a trainer at Belmont. We were down there nearly twenty years."

"Why'd you come back?"

"My dad was sick. Then when he died, he left me a couple of cottages out on Hedges Lake near Cambridge and we've been trying to sell them." As she spoke, she kept pushing her fingers through her gray hair, as if making herself more presentable now that she knew that Charlie wasn't a stranger.

"Is that where Neal is?" asked Charlie.

She didn't say anything at first, then said: "He wouldn't tell me what was wrong. I knew he was scared though. After he left, I heard about Mr. Ackerman. Neal liked Ackerman. I mean, he wasn't mixed up with his murder, if that's what you're thinking."

"I wasn't thinking anything," said Charlie, "I just want to talk to him." He kept searching Janet's face for the young face buried beneath the age and sharp lines. He wondered what she saw in his own face. She looked like

41

she'd had a difficult time. If her husband had worked around race tracks for twenty years, he guessed she probably had.

"You have any kids?" Charlie asked.

Janet looked surprised. "A daughter. She's grown up now. Last I heard she was living in Omaha."

"How do I get to this cottage?"

She stood by the sink, rubbing her left arm with her right hand as if she were cold. "Don't let him know I told you, don't even let him know you've seen me." She paused again, raised her shoulders, then let them drop. "Go north on Route 22 from Cambridge, then turn left just before Dead Lake, then take your first right. After about a mile, you'll come to a bunch of cottages on the water side of the lake. Neal will be in the seventh one. It's red with a screened-in porch. You can't miss it."

"What kind of car is he driving?"

"He's got a motorcycle: a red Honda 750."

"What's he been doing out there?"

"He said he was going to do some painting." She paused and walked over to a yellow Formica table. She wore fluffy blue slippers that made a scratching noise on the linoleum floor. "He said he was going to call me, but he hasn't. I don't know, just don't tell him I said a word."

"Is there a phone out there?"

"No."

"Does he drink?"

"Not any more."

"Why do you think something was bothering him?"

"He was jumpy, that's all. Maybe he'd been working too hard."

"That's not enough of a reason."

The woman shrugged. She had narrow, pointy shoulders

42

and Charlie couldn't imagine anyone embracing them or, as he once had, desiring to embrace them. "He had a gun in his bureau drawer. It's not there now. He must have taken it with him."

6

"SO THIS GUY, see, he was a druggist and one Sunday I popped by his house to see how he was doin. We were friends, right? So I get there and troop up the steps like some little bimbo sellin Girl Scout cookies and just as I'm raising my hand to hammer away at his door I catch a glimpse through a gap in the curtains as to what's goin on inside. Charlie, I tell you, it changed my life."

"What was it?" asked Charlie. He had asked Victor to come with him out to Hedges Lake. Charlie was driving his yellow Volkswagen and they had just passed through the small town of Greenwich. It was noon and hot and after they saw Claremon, Charlie had promised he would buy Victor lunch at the hotel in Cambridge which claimed to have invented pie a la mode. Victor liked pie a la mode.

"There was my buddy," Victor continued, "sittin in the middle of the living room floor wearin nothing but a huge diaper and holdin a baby bottle with one of those rubber nipples. Standin above him is a frau I take to be his wife. She's dressed up like a nurse with a little peaked white cap and she's shaking a finger at him, you know, scoldin him. Well, he drops his bottle and begins to bawl. This guy, he's fifty if he's a day and while he doesn't have much more

44

hair than a baby, neither does a baby have a walrus moustache."

"What'd you do?" asked Charlie.

"Like an Arab, I packed up my tents and tiptoed away.
Never told him I'd come visitin and never went again. Now
and then we'd meet for a beer, but it wasn't the same. That
diaper was always on the table between us, so to speak.
Anyway, maybe it was like that with Ackerman."

"I don't follow you," said Charlie. Sometimes he felt
destined to be dragged along after Victor's monologues
like a cat on a leash. Looking ahead, he saw the Green
Mountains rising over the green fields and white Victorian
farmhouses. Charlie downshifted at a sharp left curve. In
front of the Easton Volunteer Fire Department, a small
collie dog prepared to dash out at the Volkswagen, then fell
to scratching itself.

"Jesus, Charlie, what I been sayin is that maybe Ackerman led some secret life that nobody knew about and maybe
whoever bumped him off was tied into that life. I mean, I
can't picture Ackerman in diapers, but it could of been, you
know, anything. Like where did he go Tuesday night after
he ditched Krause? You gotta admit that's suspicious.
Think of all the people that go loopy over rubber raincoats.
Maybe there's a connection. You're the hotshot investigator,
get crackin."

"I'm not investigating anything."

"Yeah, well, what're you doin drivin thirty miles out to
some lake? Just soakin up the summer sun?"

Charlie had to admit Victor had a point. "I want to find
out why Claremon hasn't come to work."

Even as he said this, Charlie felt vaguely hypocritical
since he had never told Victor that Claremon felt it necessary to take a gun out to the cottage.

"Well, maybe I'm just a dumb, old ex-haberdasher and ex-New York super, but if I was investigatin who knocked off Mr. Ackerman, who was the only man of breeding I've come across up here in this two-bit horse hole, present company excepted, I'd try to find out what he did that Tuesday night." Victor leaned back, linked his hands behind his head, and stretched. He wore a gray sweat shirt that matched his gray fluffy hair, and a pair of gray work pants. He often dressed like this and Charlie thought it made him look like a small rain cloud. Victor looked out the window and began to whistle a phrase from "Camptown Races."

"Nice country around here," he said. "By the way, you scored yet with that waitress from the Backstretch?"

With slight irritation, Charlie wondered if there was something particularly interesting about his life which attracted people's attention or if all people had to put up with such scrutiny. As a shy man, Charlie often asked questions because he couldn't think of anything else to say; but while Victor might have problems, Charlie felt that shyness wasn't one of them.

"We've gone out to dinner once," he said. "She says she doesn't want to get involved with anyone until her divorce is settled."

"You meet her in the Backstretch? Is that why you hang out in that dump?"

"No, I met her before that. I mean, I didn't actually meet her, but I saw her."

Charlie didn't feel like explaining this so he shut up. He had first seen Doris Bailes walking through Congress Park near the Canfield Casino. Not that he had really seen that much of her. It had been late November and snowing and Doris had been wearing a heavy green down jacket with a hood. It was fresh snow and theirs were the first tracks. Charlie had gone out to see what had happened to the ducks

46

in the pond surrounding the bandstand. For several weeks, their swimming space had been decreasing as each day the pond froze a little more. The previous day the five ducks had been limited to an area six feet across. This particular morning the pond had been completely frozen and the ducks were gone, whether caught beneath the surface or rescued Charlie never knew. In their place, as it were, had been this woman walking along the perimeter of the pond. As she passed Charlie, she had said, "Good morning," in a businesslike way and continued on without slowing. If she had slowed, Charlie would have asked her about the ducks; but since she didn't, he only stared after her departing figure. As he watched, the woman stopped and lay down in the snow. At first Charlie thought she might be sick, then he saw she was making a snow angel. After a moment, she got up, looked at the indentation and walked on just as businesslike. Charlie had started to follow her, but halted at the snow angel, which he had studied for a long time. Some days later he discovered she worked at the Backstretch.

Victor shook his head and made a clucking noise with his tongue. "Look, Charlie, you won't get anywhere bein a nice guy. The truth is broads don't even like nice guys. You've got to give her a line that makes you entirely different from any dumbo in her past. You know that woman you saw me hassling last week at the Triple Crown? The one that walked out?"

Charlie remembered an attractive woman in her early forties. "What about her?"

"Just that she finally saw things my way, but believe me, I couldn't just shimmer all over like a good soldier until she decided to sleep with me for the pure virtue of the act, no, I had to make myself verbally enticing."

"What'd you say?" Charlie didn't believe that he himself could ever be verbally enticing.

"Told her that I had cancer, that I had maybe two months to live."

"You serious?"

"God's truth."

"What's going to happen when she sees you still walking around?"

"I don't know," said Victor, scratching his chin, "but whatever I say, it should be good for another date."

Cambridge, like Greenwich, was another heavily treed town of white Victorian and Colonial houses, but while the stores in Greenwich suffered economically from being too close to Saratoga, Cambridge seemed to be thriving. Charlie turned north on Route 22 and in five more minutes had reached the turnoff before Dead Lake.

The cottages bordering Hedges Lake were small and packed together. Victor counted them off in his Lawrence Welk voice and at the seventh one, Charlie pulled over and cut the engine.

Neal Claremon's cottage appeared deserted: windows closed, curtains drawn. It seemed to have about three rooms while attached to the front was a large screened porch which ran the width of the cottage. About ten feet of sand separated it from its neighbors. The cottage had been painted bright red and attached to the roof of the porch was a white sign with the words: "Home At Last." Charlie knocked on the porch door. There was no answer.

"Nobody home there," shouted a voice. Charlie turned to see a man half leaning out of a gable window of the cottage to his right. "Nobody been there since Saturday."

Charlie nodded, opened the screen door, walked across the porch to the front door and knocked again. There was no answer. On the porch was an old brown sofa and two overstuffed chairs, as well as some aluminum lawn chairs.

Charlie tried the door. It was locked. The window in its center was covered with a blue curtain and he couldn't see around it.

"I just told you, there's nobody home," called the man next door. "You ever hear of criminal trespass?" The head disappeared and Charlie assumed the man was coming downstairs. The small lake was ringed with cottages. Out on the water, at least a dozen motorboats were towing water skiers. Charlie went around the left side of the cottage and began trying to look through windows. Victor followed him.

"You'd think that furniture on the porch would get wet," Victor said.

Through a crack beneath the shade of a kitchen window, Charlie saw a box of Ritz Crackers and a wedge of moldy cheese. The rest of the windows seemed to be completely covered by curtains, but then, on the right side of the house, Charlie found a living room window where the curtain had been folded back against the sill, leaving an opening about the size of his thumb. Charlie knelt down beside it, but even with this small peephole, the room was still too dark to see anything.

"Victor, get my flashlight from the car."

"Shonuff, bossman."

A door slammed next door and a portly man of about fifty in tartan plaid Bermuda shorts and a yellow and green striped shirt came bustling toward them. "I told you and told you," he said, "there's nobody home. You gonna leave or am I gonna call the cops?"

As Charlie straightened up, his attention was caught by the man's sneakers which were white with the word "disco" printed all over them in different kinds of lettering. "Neal Claremon works for me," he said, "and I want to know where he is."

"Could of fooled me. You don't look like Ackerman, you don't look like a dead man. You think I'm dumb or something?"

Charlie took a business card from his wallet. "I'm Charles Bradshaw, chief of security, Lorelei Stables. This is my assistant, Victor Plotz."

Victor clicked his heels together as he handed Charlie the flashlight.

"You want to call the police," said Charlie, "then go ahead. When was the last time you saw Claremon?" Charlie knelt down to the space between the curtain and windowsill, trying to keep his eye to the hole and shine the light in the room at the same time.

"Claremon was around on Saturday, said he had some painting to do. Why you peeking through that window?"

But Charlie didn't answer. He had seen a tiny portion of the wheel of a motorcycle and something else that made him get up and walk rapidly around the corner of the cottage and across the screened porch to the front door. It never occurred to him that he ought to call the police. For a moment, he forgot he wasn't a policeman himself. Turning slightly and balancing on his left foot, he kicked the door a little below the knob. The glass rattled, but the door stayed shut.

"Here now," shouted the man with disco sneakers, "that's private property."

Charlie ignored him and kicked again harder. This time the door sprung open, swung around and hit the wall with a crash. Through the door, almost leaping through it Charlie thought later, came the sweet, heavy smell of decomposing flesh. Charlie caught his breath, then groped around the corner for a light switch, found one, and flicked it on. What he saw, he had seen many times in his twenty years as a policeman, but even after this long he couldn't see a corpse without wanting to throw up. He turned back to the man from next door.

"You want the police? Then call them. Make sure you also call Chief Peterson in Saratoga. Give him my name and tell him he should get out here."

Without waiting for the man's response, Charlie turned back to the open doorway. Victor started to walk across the porch, then sniffed, then stopped.

"I know what's in there," he said, "but if you think I'm going to take a look, you're wackola."

There was no furniture in the room and the walls had recently been painted white. Mixed with the smell of rotting flesh was the smell of fresh paint. A man whom Charlie assumed to be Neal Claremon lay on his stomach near the opening to the kitchen. He wore only a dark blue bathing suit with white trim and in his back were six red holes. He was a small man and very thin and lay sprawled on the floor as if he had been dropped there. Nearly the entire floor was covered with a partially dried layer of his blood. It had been the blood which Charlie had caught a glimpse of through the window. With his left arm flung forward and his right arm reaching back, Claremon appeared to be swimming through it. Parked in the middle of this red lake was a bright red motorcycle.

7

"I STILL DON'T SEE what reason you had kicking open the door, Charlie. I mean, any way you cut it that amounts to interfering with police business."

Charlie stuck his hands in his pockets and glanced out at the lake where it seemed even more people were now water-skiing. As he looked, an attractive woman in a yellow bikini shot by Claremon's small dock and waved at the policemen. "There was no way of knowing Claremon was dead," Charlie said lamely.

"After five days what the hell you figure he's doing there on the floor? Humping a board?" Peterson put his hands on his hips and grinned at Charlie. It wasn't a pleasant grin. He was a tall man, about three or four inches over six feet, who liked to accentuate his height by bouncing on his toes. As usual, he wore a three-piece blue suit with a silver chain across his large stomach. Peterson was about forty-five, had thick, black hair, and a hoarse voice. People said he looked more like a senator than a police chief. Actually, his title was Director of Public Safety, but to most people he was simply Chief.

"It seemed best to find out," said Charlie.

"Why'd you come out here in the first place?"

"I told you, we're shorthanded at the stable. Claremon had called in sick. I thought he was out here drinking."

There were a dozen police cars from the State Police, Cambridge police, sheriff's department, Salem and Greenwich police, plus two cars from Saratoga. Four or five of the policemen were holding back a crowd of gawkers dressed mostly in bathing suits, who were hoping to see the body removed. The rest of the police wandered around the outside of the cottage waiting for the arrival of the State Police lab crew. Charlie guessed the case would be handled by the State Police and the Washington County sheriff's department. In any event, Peterson was basically a visitor.

Charlie and Peterson stood near the right-hand corner of the porch. Through the front door of the cottage, Charlie could see Claremon's blood in the bright living room light as if the blood itself were a beacon which had drawn together policemen and gawkers alike. The only person who appeared uninterested was Victor Plotz who had taken off his shoes and was sitting at the end of Claremon's dock dabbling his feet in the water.

Although the various policemen were certainly serious and even somber, Charlie detected that element of vindication which he had observed before on similar occasions, as if the police felt energized by this fresh example of foul behavior: behavior which once more proved their importance to the community. It made him again grateful that he had quit his job with the Saratoga police department.

"How're you coming with the Ackerman investigation?" asked Charlie, trying to keep his voice toneless but polite.

Peterson clasped his hands behind his back and nodded to a deputy from Salem. "It's moving along. You know how it is: Bit by bit you find all the pieces. Lots of elbow grease and good luck. Had a piece of good luck last night

53

as a matter of fact. Some kid turned up the white raincoat, rain hat, and an old nylon stocking in a garage about two blocks from the YMCA."

"Can you trace it?" asked Charlie.

"Nah, it's old stuff. Came from Sears. I gotta man on it, but it looks like a dead end."

"What did ballistics say about the gun?"

"Seems to have been a European jobby, a .9mm." Peterson looked disapprovingly at Charlie. He had thick black eyebrows which Charlie suspected he brushed down to make him look more foreboding. "Just what's your interest in the matter?" he asked.

"Lew was my friend and I worked for him."

"Well, you know, we're following up a number of leads. I can't say we've got anything definite yet, but on the other hand I think we've covered a lot of ground."

Charlie, who had heard Peterson deliver speeches like this hundreds of times, found himself clenching his teeth. Glancing away, he caught the eye of Claremon's chubby neighbor, whose name had turned out to be Patrick Truesdale. The man wore an expression of superior gloating and it occurred to Charlie that Truesdale thought he was being arrested.

"Do you plan to arrest Field?" asked Charlie abruptly.

Peterson raised himself on tiptoe and balanced there a second before dropping back down. "Charlie, I can't possibly discuss such matters, I mean, how can you think . . . ."

"Do you have evidence against him?"

"How can you think I would reveal . . . ."

"What do you plan to do about Claremon?"

"As far as I can tell, it's not my case."

Looking away, Charlie tried to define his mood to himself. He felt frustrated and angry, but he wasn't sure why.

He hoped it simply wasn't a matter of having his feelings hurt because Peterson wouldn't confide in him. Glancing toward the lake, he saw Victor skimming stones into the water.

"Claremon worked for Ackerman five days," Charlie said. "He was a loner who Ackerman hired himself. A groom described Claremon to me as nervous and jumpy. Anyway, the minute he learns that Ackerman was shot he comes here to hide out. Not only that, he brings a gun. Later that day, somebody comes and shoots him with a silenced revolver. Not only that, but I bet ballistics will show you it was the same gun that killed Ackerman, your .9mm European jobby."

"How do you know the gun had a silencer?"

"He was shot six times. You think one of these neighbors wouldn't have telephoned? Talk to that guy over there in the striped shirt and see if he heard anything or if Claremon had any visitors."

"You know, Charlie, you're taking a lot of liberties for a private citizen."

There was a stirring in the crowd as the ambulance arrived followed by the State Police lab crew in a blue van. Charlie watched them walk toward the cottage, cross the screened porch, then stop at the door as they realized they couldn't walk into the room without walking through Claremon's blood. One of the ambulance attendants ran to the blue van, took five pair of black rubbers from the back and ran back to the other men on the porch. The five men pulled on the rubbers, then delicately entered the cottage on tiptoe.

"I'm not taking liberties," said Charlie. "I'm just pointing out some information that you might find useful. I'll be telling exactly the same stuff to the State Police and I thought you might like to get the jump on them before they come and start telling you your job."

An hour later Charlie was driving back to Saratoga with Victor. Although it was nearly four o'clock and he hadn't eaten, he didn't feel hungry. Both had decided against pie a la mode at the Cambridge hotel: Charlie because his stomach didn't feel like it and Victor out of sympathy. Later Charlie wanted to go swimming, put in his half mile, but he doubted he would get the time. He found himself on edge as if there were crumbs in his bed or his shoes were too tight. He kept thinking of Claremon's living room as he had last seen it, filled with high-power lights, while lab men tiptoed around dusting for fingerprints. He had watched the ambulance attendants roll Claremon clumsily onto a stretcher. His eyes had been open and his expression was one of faint surprise, as if he'd just understood the punch line of a joke. Then they had covered him with a red blanket and carried him out to the satisfaction of the waiting crowd. Several people in bathing suits had taken photographs, while one woman carefully pointed out what was happening to twin girls in a stroller.

Afterward, Charlie talked to a State Police lieutenant he had known for about fifteen years, as well as a Washington County deputy with whom he occasionally went trout fishing in the Battenkill. Both had been friendlier than Peterson, but Charlie felt ill at ease and cut off. After describing Claremon's connection with Ackerman, Charlie wanted to give some suggestions as to what they might look for, but the lieutenant politely made it clear they neither wanted nor sought his advice. Basically, Charlie was a private citizen, an outsider.

Out at the lake, Victor had mostly stayed out of the way,

56

except for posing for some photographs as the-man-who-found-the-body. As they rode back to Saratoga, he whistled bits of songs to himself and looked out the window. Charlie couldn't tell if he was thinking or just letting his mind ride empty.

"So whatcha going to do now?" said Victor at last.

"What do you mean?"

"Are you going to investigate or not investigate?"

"I can't do anything, Victor . . . ."

"Vic."

"Sure, sure, but look, I'm a stable guard. I just can't go barging around."

"You're chief of security of Lorelei Stables."

Charlie glanced at Victor to see if he was serious, then looked back barely in time to avoid a tractor which was pulling out onto the road. Victor gave the finger to the kid driving the tractor.

"Vic, that means nothing. It's like saying I'm king of the moon."

"You got five guards workin under you. Make 'em help."

"It's not my business. Let the cops do it."

"So what do you feel like doin right now? I mean, you want to get a few beers and cruise the drive-ins?"

"No thanks, I've got to break the news to Claremon's wife. Peterson would make a mess of it."

"You goin to ask her any questions about her husband?"

"I might."

"I see," said Victor. He pulled the collar of his gray sweat shirt out past his chin, blew down the opening several times, then began fanning his face with his hand. "So perhaps it could be said," he continued, "that while you're not exactly investigating, you are investigating more than you were this morning. Right?"

Charlie looked out across the rolling pastures spotted

with dairy cows. Many of the hills were topped with trees and in the distance he could see the hazy beginnings of the Adirondacks. He told himself he liked this countryside better than any other and he knew that Ackerman had felt the same way.

"That's right," he said at last.

8

CHARLIE STOPPED his Volkswagen in front of Claremon's house on Maple Avenue and cut the engine, but instead of getting out he sat with his hands on the wheel. He had dropped Victor off uptown, saying he might meet him that evening at the Backstretch.

Looking up Maple Avenue, Charlie could see a small white house which his mother had rented about ten years before; see another house where a girl had lived whom he had once had a crush on, a girl later killed when she was thrown by a horse; see a house where six brothers lived whom Charlie had coached in Little League baseball. It often seemed to Charlie that his memories were realer than the flickering present that appeared to surround him. As he sat in his car on this Wednesday afternoon in late July, he felt the presence of those past days like seeing different colored threads in a piece of fabric.

Ackerman too had been interested in the past and, partly because of Charlie's encouragement, had begun reading about Saratoga history the same time Charlie had begun to swim at the Y. Most recently Ackerman had begun to study Richard Canfield, the prince of Saratoga gamblers who had closed his casino in 1907 to concentrate on his art collection. Ackerman had been drawn to Canfield, because both men had freed themselves from the poverty of their youth by running poker games in their teens and early twenties. But while Canfield had gone on to build greater and greater casinos, Ackerman had turned to horses, giving up all other types of gambling which he claimed were close to robbery. Canfield had always been honest in telling people that if they gambled they would lose; but he argued against the intermittent closing of the casinos by reformers by saying, "They gambled in the Garden of Eden and they will again if there's another one."

Ackerman had quoted this to Charlie several weeks before, and had added, "That may be true of Eden, but it won't happen here. Gambling ruins a town."

They had been sitting in Ackerman's office at the stable and Frank Warner had chosen that moment to come in to discuss a nervous horse that required a goat tethered in its stall to keep it calm. Charlie wanted to ask Ackerman if he thought there was any chance of a resumption of gambling in Saratoga, but he had never been able to get back to it. Sitting in his Volkswagen in front of Neal Claremon's house, he wondered if he ought to have gotten back to it. But there were dozens of half-completed conversations with Ackerman which he had thought they would have plenty of time to finish. This in fact became another aspect of his grief: that he hadn't had time to ask Ackerman about some horse or book or ask his advice about some problem with his swimming or tell him of a crooked gambler he had been reading about: John North who had been lynched by vigilantes in Vicksburg and whose roulette wheel had been "tied up to his dangling body" as a caution to other gamblers.

One of the pains of Ackerman being dead was that Charlie kept vividly remembering him in all the situations he had ever known him, making it seem as if he were

60

haunted by dozens of Ackermans. As Charlie got out of his car, he realized he had a similar problem with Mrs. Claremon.

It was difficult to think of the woman inside the small renovated garage as the middle-aged wife of the man whose body he had discovered at Hedges Lake and also as the girl who had sat next to him in typing class. Yet his memory of seeing Mrs. Claremon that morning was no more vivid than his memories of Janet Macomb in typing class, and now Charlie had to go in and tell little Janet Macomb that her husband had been shot six times in the back. Well, better him than that fool Peterson.

Charlie crossed the sidewalk, stepping over and around the kiddy debris—tipped-over tricycle, pots and kitchen utensils, tin pail and shovel—to the front door, and knocked. Janet Macomb or Mrs. Claremon, both names registered equally in Charlie's mind, must have been watching because she opened the door immediately.

Looking at her, Charlie searched her narrow face for traces of the younger girl and although he found them in her eyes and cheekbones, it still seemed as if Janet Macomb were wearing a mask like those Japanese theater masks he had once seen on television.

"I'd like to talk to you," he said.

Janet stood back and Charlie walked past her to the kitchen which was bright and sunny and didn't have the living room's cheap pine panelling which Charlie hated. Janet followed but stopped in the doorway with her hand on the frame as Charlie turned and looked at her. He knew she could tell something was wrong.

"I'm sorry to have to do this to you," Charlie said, "but your husband's been killed." As soon as he had uttered the words, Charlie judged himself for saying the wrong ones; but he had broken this sort of news to the survivors many

many times and each time he judged himself for not doing it carefully enough, although he didn't know how he could ever say it to make it all right.

Janet Claremon didn't appear to react. She looked down at the floor. Then, for a moment, she seemed smaller to Charlie. Even her blue checked gingham dress now seemed too big for her, as if she were trying to draw in her body, reduce it to the smallest possible size. The sun came in through the window over the kitchen sink, making the yellow Formica table sparkle.

"Was it the motorcycle?" she said at last.

"He was shot. The police will come and tell you about it, but I wanted to tell you first."

"Why would anyone shoot him?"

"The police don't know."

She looked at him briefly with large brown eyes, then looked away again. "What happened?"

"I don't know either. I found him in the cottage. He'd been shot several times in the back. Apparently he's been dead for a few days."

"You mean he's just been lying out there?"

Charlie nodded.

Janet walked slowly to a wooden chair by the table and sat down. She noticed a spot on the yellow Formica and began to pick at it. Her fingernails were long and red, and Charlie remembered that years before she had worried that typing would damage them.

"Do you mind if I ask you some questions about your husband?" said Charlie. He went to the sink, filled a glass with water, and handed it to Janet, who took the glass and set it down without drinking.

"I guess not."

"Do you know why he was frightened?"

She dipped her fingers in the glass of water and touched

62

them to her eyes. As if she were giving herself tears, thought Charlie.

"No, I asked him what was wrong, but he wouldn't say. He could be awfully touchy."

"How long had he seemed frightened?"

"I don't know, maybe I noticed it about ten days ago. But he wasn't really frightened, just that something was bothering him. When he heard Mr. Ackerman had been killed, that's when he really seemed frightened."

Charlie leaned against the sink and looked over at the small woman sitting at the table. It was almost with surprise that he realized he was asking her questions which were basically none of his business. "Had your husband known Ackerman a long time?" he asked.

"I don't think so, at least he never mentioned him before. He must of known who he was though. I mean you couldn't spend twenty years working at race tracks and not know who he was."

"Who did your husband work for before Ackerman?"

"Mr. Dwyer. First down on Long Island for ten years, then up here."

"Why did he leave?"

"I don't know. I mean, I don't know if he quit or was fired. Sometimes he just wouldn't talk, but I know he was upset when he left and I know he liked Mr. Dwyer."

"When did he leave Dwyer?"

"A little over two weeks ago."

Robert Dwyer had been at the track for as long as Charlie could remember. He had a stable on the west side of Saratoga, across the highway from the Saratoga Spa State Park. He also had property on Long Island and a farm in Kentucky. Although Charlie knew who he was, he'd never actually spoken to him. He knew, however, that he'd been friends with Ackerman and that Dwyer had given Ackerman a lot of help when the younger man began to buy and train horses. From what Charlie had heard, Dwyer had turned over much of the control of his stable to his son-in-law, Wayne Curry. Dwyer had had a stroke some years before and was still confined to a wheelchair. Whenever Charlie saw him in public—at a concert at the Performing Arts Center or at a restaurant—he was always being wheeled by Curry. It was the son-in-law, Charlie remembered, who pushed Dwyer forward when he delivered the eulogy at Ackerman's funeral, and had then stood the whole time as if at attention.

"And your husband said nothing that would give you any idea why he left Dwyer's stable?" said Charlie.

"No, I asked him, but he ignored me. Sometimes, when things were bothering him, he'd go out on his motorcycle. He did that a lot after he left Dwyer."

Charlie watched her sit with her hands in her lap. She was so thin that he could see the sharp points where her bones pressed against the fabric of her dress. Although he guessed she hadn't had much of a marriage, he was sorry her husband had been killed and wished her pain was like a cloak so he could lift it from her. That he had once had a slight crush on her didn't matter. Charlie had always been prone to useless crushes and sometimes it seemed that half the women in Saratoga had at one time or other unwittingly received his attention.

Along with Charlie's sorrow at the death of Janet's husband, he felt angry that there was somebody around who thought he could just erase people as if they were no more than a smudge on a blackboard. And although he didn't, like Jack Krause, wish he could destroy this person himself, he wished that Peterson could somehow blossom into the perfect policeman he had never shown himself to be in the past.

"Is there anything I can do for you?" asked Charlie.

"No, you've been very kind. I just need some time by myself, I guess."

"You have enough money?"

She nodded but didn't speak.

Charlie considered asking her not to tell Peterson that he had been there, instead he said, "Will you call me if you remember anything your husband might have said about why he was frightened or why he left Dwyer's stable?" He gave her his card and wrote his home phone number on it.

She nodded again, then said, "Are you working with the police?"

"No," said Charlie, "I've nothing to do with the police."

9

"NOW LOOK ME in the eye," said Victor leaning over
the bar, "the reason you won't be Charlie's girl is that
you're stuck on me. Is that right?" Then he laughed and
scratched his head.

Doris Bailes set his drink down before him. "I just can't
resist men with hair like dirty cotton candy," she said.

"Dirty hair, clean heart," said Victor. He was sitting on
a stool at the Backstretch waiting for Charlie. It was just
past six and Victor was beginning on his third vodka
collins. Doris had come to work a few minutes before and
now Victor was trying to get her going, as he expressed it
to himself. At the end of the bar, the young blond stripper
was waiting for the Chinese restaurant to close so she could
begin work.

"See here," said Victor, "you come over to my place and
I'll show you my tattoo."

"Why can't you show me here?" Doris had begun wash-
ing glasses, and the steam from the hot water tap made
her cheeks turn red. She wore a white blouse and jeans.
Around her neck was a thin gold chain.

"Not private enough."

"Is it dirty?"

"No, but I'm the only guy you'll ever meet with a picture

of President Nixon tattooed on his ass. What the hell, it was cheaper than the butterfly. You like cats? You could come over and see my cat. He's only got one eye. Or I could show you my swatch collection."

"Your what?"

"Swatches. You know, samples of fabric. Started collecting them when I sold men's clothing, then stopped when I got fired. Must have over a thousand. Seemed a shame to throw them out. Would you like them?"

"What would I do with them?"

Victor shrugged. Although he took pleasure in cracking wise, as he called it, he knew he was becoming a little maniacal. But the discovery of Claremon's body that afternoon had unnerved him; and whenever he thought of it, he could see that awful red cottage; and even though he had refrained from looking at the body, his imagination was doing its best to invent its own grisly picture. In any case, he enjoyed talking to Doris Bailes. Not that he would actually make a pass at her, but he liked how she seemed to be her own person. Victor, who knew he had a tendency to act up a little—he wouldn't go so far as to call it showing off—felt that Doris would always be consistent, behaving the same way before a crowd of people or by herself.

"Tell me the truth," asked Victor, "are you sweet on some third party?"

Doris pushed her brown hair out of her eyes with the back of one hand. "I'm not sweet on anyone at the moment. Why can't I just be happy by myself? It's cheaper that way, safer too."

"You're too pretty for that. Maybe you're holdin the torch for some guy in prison or some guy in the army who right now is slogging his way through the Georgia swamps. You know what they say, lovin keeps you young."

"Is that what keeps you so young?"

"You better believe it. I got skin like a baby. But seriously, why won't you let Charlie fall to one knee and pop the question: decent guy, steady habits, reads books, doesn't snore. If I wasn't committed to broads, I'd take up with him myself."

Doris raised her eyebrows. "You'd look cute on a dance floor." Then she paused and asked: "You think Charlie will investigate Ackerman's murder?"

"Where'd you hear that?"

"A groom from Ackerman's stable was in here talking about it."

Victor drank some of his drink. "News gets around, right? Charlie don't know it yet, but he's hot on the scent. That Peterson, he's on the case nearly a week and nothin happens. Charlie takes over and right the first day he finds another murder. Now that's what I call investigatin." Victor described driving out to Hedges Lake and finding Claremon's body. He also wanted to say how he felt when he saw the ambulance attendants hurry out with the body on the stretcher covered with a red blanket, but he couldn't find the right words.

"It must have been terrible."

"Yeah, I been feelin queasy all day. Give me another one of those vodka collinses, will you?"

As she made his drink, Victor looked at the photographs of boxers: Billy Conn, Gorilla Jones, Fritzie Zivic. He didn't recognize the names, but figured Charlie must know who they were. Actually, Victor had never been much of a boxing fan. It was too clean. Wrestling was what he liked, Australian tag teams. But mostly he didn't like sports, didn't like just watching things, although years before he had enjoyed bird watching, but that had been when his kid was little and things were easier. Victor still had on his gray sweat shirt. Continuing to look at the boxers on the wall, he reached his right hand down through his collar and scratched his chest.

Doris handed him his drink. "Does Charlie have any ideas about who might have killed Ackerman?"

"Yeah, he must have. You know Charlie though, he stays pretty quiet about what he's thinking. But I'll tell you something: last Tuesday night Ackerman ditched his bodyguard and went off by himself. Now I'm not sure if that's a clue or evidence or suspicious or what the fuck you want to call it, but I find it interesting."

"What if I told you he was in here?"

"You're kidding."

"I'm sure it was Tuesday," said Doris, "because I had a trotter that won that night and I bought everyone at the bar a drink. Ackerman had a straight tomato juice."

Doris stood with her hands on the bar facing Victor. The way she squinted her eyes as she remembered reminded Victor of a cashier who had worked with him at the men's clothing store on Madison. In those days, Victor had been firmly married and never drank. He had never even fantasized about this woman until years later, long after she had quit and he'd been fired.

"You mean Ackerman ditched his bodyguard," said Victor, "just so he could come here and drink tomato juice? He must of been sweet on you too."

Doris shook her head. "No, he must have been someplace else as well, because he came in around ten o'clock and stayed about fifteen minutes."

"Did he come here often?"

"Maybe every couple of months. I've never really talked to him, although I recognized him of course. He was a handsome man."

"What'd he act like? Think he'd been seein a broad?"

"I don't think so. He seemed angry. I said a few words to

69

him and although he wasn't exactly unfriendly, he seemed preoccupied."

"How d'you mean? Did he act funny in some way?"

"No, I mean, he was usually pretty friendly and that night, I don't know, he seemed quiet and angry. He didn't talk to anyone. Just sat at the bar and drank his tomato juice."

"I'd feel better if you'd seen him kick a cat. Did he say anything about what he was doing over here?"

Another customer had come in and Doris paused to draw him a beer. Victor watched her figure as she walked away and decided it was time to call up one of his girlfriends. The sooner the better. When Doris came back, he said, "You still joggin? Say, I wasn't jokin about showin you that tattoo. It shows Nixon with that little dog of his. The dog's a real knockout. Okay, okay, tell me about Ackerman."

"It wasn't much. I asked him what he was doing over here and he said he had some stuff to take care of."

"Stuff?"

"That's what he said."

"You know how he was getting around since Krause wasn't there to drive him?"

"I don't know how he got here, but one of the regulars gave him a ride home."

"Yeah, who's that?"

"A stooper by the name of Wally Berrigan."

"A what?"

"A stooper, you know, someone that picks up tickets at the track, hoping to find a winning one that someone's dropped."

"Seems like a great way to earn a living. Have any idea where he lives?"

"In a rooming house on Phila, just past Lena's." Lena's

was a coffee shop that had folk music on the weekends. "I've seen him sitting on the front porch."

"Maybe I'll have a word with him," said Victor. "Do me a favor, will you, don't tell Charlie about this."

"Why not?" She tilted her head slightly as she looked at him. Victor thought it made her look like an intelligent bird. Nothing like an owl. Maybe some kind of partridge or grouse. Anyway, it was a bird he liked.

"I want to surprise him," he said.

10

AS HE DROVE DOWN the northeastern shore of Saratoga Lake, Charlie thought it must have been along here that Old Smoke Morrissey had built the grandstands from which people could watch the boat races he had introduced during the Civil War. Thousands had come to see the international amateur races and then, later on, the intercollegiate regattas. In the evening, sportsmen could continue their quest for action in Old Smoke's casino: an activity from which women and the male residents of Saratoga Springs had been barred.

Charlie wondered if it had been common to exclude town residents from the casinos. He knew that Richard Canfield had kept townspeople out of his casino in the nineties and had been closed Sundays as well in an effort to placate the reformists. Presumably residents, including women, could bet in at least some of the other twenty gambling houses. Charlie recalled that the owner of the track at the time, Gottfried Walbaum, had had a special room where women and children could bet and lose their money in private.

Charlie was sorry that the popularity of boat racing had declined. This evening the lake was spotted with speedboats and sailboats, and Charlie regretted he knew nothing of the professional scullers of the past. He sighed and turned his attention back to the road.

He had decided it was time to see Ackerman's partner, Harvey Field; and instead of meeting Victor at the Backstretch, Charlie was driving out to Field's house on Saratoga Lake. He felt nervous about this, because Field himself made Charlie nervous. He had a sepulchral presence: the sort of man you didn't hear enter a room or see leaving it. He was a small man with light gray eyes and looking at you it seemed he didn't really see you but was looking through to some other place. Charlie had no idea what Field thought of him, no idea if he even knew who Charlie was. Field was the man who handled the money, and among Ackerman's diverse friends and acquaintances, Charlie thought Field one of the strangest.

Charlie also felt nervous, because he knew he had no business to see Field. So far he didn't think of himself as investigating Ackerman's death as much as stumbling into situations which gave him information about that death. But seeing Field was a definite act in his stumbling investigation.

Field lived on a cliff above the lake and the house was approached by a winding, tree-lined driveway marked with signs saying, Private Drive, No Trespassing. Charlie turned left, shifting his Volkswagen into second as he began to climb the hill. He told himself that he also wanted to settle in his mind once and for all whether Field was mixed up with Ackerman's death. If Charlie decided he wasn't involved, then he wanted to ask Field if he would back him in his own investigation. That too made him nervous.

Reaching the top of the hill, Charlie parked by the triple garage door. It was a long, single-story white house with picture windows. In the backyard was a dog run surrounded by a high chain link fence. The dog run seemed almost as long as the house itself. In the front, a sloping yard ran down about one hundred yards to the first trees, giving a panoramic view of the lake. Charlie walked around to the front door. Finding no bell, he knocked. It was a large red door with a small bronze plate with the name "Field" engraved on it. Charlie could hear cars passing down on the road, birds fluttering and chirping among the bushes, and from inside a noise which sounded like growling. It was a warm evening, but the air was so clear he could pick out individual trees on the other side of the lake. Charlie had on his tan suit, and as he waited he tugged at his cuffs and smoothed down his tie.

The door was opened abruptly by a short, round Oriental with black hair cut like a helmet. The man might have been fifty or ninety. "You want?" he said.

"I'd like to see Mr. Field," said Charlie. He gave the man one of the cards that said he was chief of security at Lorelei Stables. The man was about five feet tall and, while not actually as wide as he was high, he gave that impression. He wore a dark suit and steel rim glasses.

"Wait, please." The man shut the door.

When he returned ten minutes later, Charlie had decided he must have interrupted Field's dinner. This made him even more uncomfortable.

"Follow, please."

The small Oriental stood aside to let Charlie enter, then closed and locked the door. The house was dark and much cooler than it had been outside. Charlie followed the man down a long, carpeted hallway with brightly colored prints on the walls. He didn't know any of the artists and some of the pictures appeared no more than squiggles. As he paused to look at a squiggle, he felt something wet touch his left hand. Glancing down, he saw a white Doberman pinscher practically enveloping his hand in its mouth. Charlie gasped

74

and jerked away, trying to pull his hand free. The dog braced itself and tightened its grip, not breaking the skin. It looked up at him calmly with pink eyes.

The man stopped when he heard Charlie make a noise. "Dog won't hurt," he said.

Charlie wanted to say, "But what about me?" Instead he only nodded, not wanting to do anything to upset the white Doberman. His hand tingled and felt wet and clammy. He imagined the Doberman burying it in the backyard. Charlie had never liked the breed, feeling they looked like a sort of sexual weapon, and the albino was probably the least attractive Doberman he had seen. Slowly, he again began to follow the Oriental. The Doberman moved at his side, keeping his hand firmly in its mouth. Because of the dimness of the hall, the white dog was like a light flickering at the corner of his eye.

The man led him to a tiny room at the back of the house furnished only with a desk, two straight chairs and a file cabinet. One window was set high in a light green wall. There were no pictures, but on the floor was a maroon rug.

"Wait here."

Charlie sat down and the dog sat down beside him, still gripping his hand. The man left without glancing at Charlie or the dog. Charlie kept looking at the dog, which looked back at him with its pink eyes. It seemed very alert and ready. Charlie knew that someone like John Wesley Hardin or one of the Dalton boys would have just hauled off and shot the dog.

Field appeared five minutes later. He seemed even thinner and smaller than Charlie remembered. He didn't look at Charlie but went to the chair behind the desk and sat down. A pair of shiny black shoes poked through from underneath.

"I don't have much time," he said. "I told Warner if there was any trouble at the stable he should handle it himself. That being the case, I don't see what you are doing here." He folded his hands in front of him on the blotter. He had on a white shirt, gray pants, and suspenders. His face was a perfect almond shape and just as wrinkled: a gray almond.

"First of all," said Charlie, "maybe you can tell your dog to let go of my hand." Charlie hadn't meant to speak so abruptly, but he was beginning to feel ill-used.

Field, who until that moment had appeared determined and businesslike, sighed and looked uncertainly at the dog. "I'll see what I can do," he said.

Reaching into his pocket, he took out a chrome-plated whistle, which Charlie recognized as an Acme Thunderer. Field raised it to his lips and blew it twice. The noise occupied the room like broken glass in a paper bag. Charlie winced and the dog winced as well but continued to keep a firm grip on Charlie's hand. Field blew the whistle several more times with no more effect than to cause a growing pain in Charlie's ears.

Field put away the whistle and stared at the dog. Then he stood up and walked around the desk. "Swaps," he said, "drop the hand. Swaps!" The dog continued to sit with Charlie's hand in its mouth, looking, Charlie thought, basically contented. Field approached the dog, dropped to one knee and tried to pry open the dog's jaws. For a few moments, Charlie's hand was wrenched this way and that until Field was at last able to force open the jaws and Charlie pulled his hand free.

Field got to his feet. "Now lie down!" The dog lay down in the center of the maroon rug and stared at Field as he returned to his chair behind the desk. When he had sat down and began to breathe more slowly, Field said, "Lew Ackerman gave me that dog. He's named after the first horse that Lew ever won money on." Field hesitated and again there was that uncertain look. "I don't know why he gave it to me. I've never liked dogs."

"Why don't you get rid of it?" asked Charlie.

Field shook his head. "I couldn't do that. Give away Lew's dog? I couldn't do it." He glanced at the dog, which was staring at him attentively with its chin on its crossed front paws. Even its nose was white and its nostrils opened and closed as it breathed. "Anyway," Field continued, "none of this explains what you're doing here."

Charlie looked at the small man, nominally his employer, sitting behind the desk. He had become fragile and comic. As he thought this, Charlie remembered his uncle once furiously pursuing a beagle puppy under the dining room table because he refused to have the dog in the room while he ate dinner. It was difficult to maintain one's dignity while chastising a dog.

"One of the grooms has been murdered," said Charlie. "A man named Neal Claremon who Lew hired about two weeks ago. I found Claremon's body this afternoon." Charlie went on to explain how Warner had thought Claremon was out drinking, how he had gone to Claremon's house and from there to Hedges Lake.

"What I was wondering," said Charlie, "was if you knew anything about Claremon or why Lew hired him?"

As he had told the story, Charlie had seen Field's face close down and become determined and businesslike so that it was impossible to guess what he was thinking. Field had very thin gray hair that was brushed back across his pink scalp. Before he spoke, he smoothed it back with his hands as if brushing cobwebs out of it.

"Certainly, I am shocked," said Field, without showing the least emotion, "but what I don't entirely understand is what this has to do with you. Presumably the police are investigating."

This was just what Charlie didn't want to hear. He stretched in his chair, took a fairly clean handkerchief from his breast pocket, and blew his nose. The white Doberman glanced at him, then looked back at Field.

"I believe," said Charlie, "that Claremon's death is connected to Lew's. I would like to discover what that connection is. Chief Peterson isn't certain there is a connection, although he may change his mind when he gets the ballistics report. Peterson believes that Lew was either murdered by some criminal out of his past or he was murdered by you."

Field sat up as if he had been jabbed. "Are you serious? Why should I kill Lew? He was my best friend."

Charlie shrugged and slowly began to fold his handkerchief. "People told him the two of you had been quarreling. Also you're somewhat mysterious, I mean, the way you live out here by yourself. You're an unknown figure and so people speculate about you."

"Just because I like my privacy . . ." Field hesitated, then continued, "I know nothing about Claremon. Lew and Warner were completely in charge of running the stable."

"I figure," said Charlie, "that Peterson will come out here this evening and ask you some questions about Claremon. Can you prove you didn't know him?"

"How would I know him? I don't even recognize the name. Okay, so Lew and I had a few quarrels, but they didn't mean anything."

"What kind of quarrels?"

"Business quarrels. They don't concern you."

"Why didn't you go to the funeral?"

Field looked away toward the dog. He seemed to Charlie one of those solitary men whose shyness and fear of human contact lead them into sad lives. On top of that, he was also a stubborn man.

"I said my goodbyes at the funeral home the previous

evening," said Field, "and I had no desire to have my hand pumped by a lot of fools. Anyway, I don't see why I have to explain myself to you."

"You don't, really. I'm just trying to give you an idea how people are thinking. As I said, people also think Lew might have been killed by some hood, somebody who had known him before and maybe recently got out of prison."

Field shook his head. "Lew knew all kinds of people, but they liked him. He wasn't killed by hoods."

"In that case," said Charlie, "that makes you even more suspect. I mean, if he was either killed by hoods or by you and we take away the hoods, what's left?"

"But I tell you he was my friend," said Field, raising his voice. "I'd known him nearly thirty years."

"How'd you first meet him?" asked Charlie. He had noticed that Field had red splotches of flaky skin on the backs of his hands. Now, as he talked, Field began to pick at them.

"I was an accountant in New York, quite a young man. Lew started talking to me in a restaurant one day at lunchtime. It turned out he had a poker game and supported himself by playing cards. He wasn't even twenty at the time. Finally he asked me if I wanted to invest in him, I don't know, put up a stake of five hundred dollars. We'd been talking about two hours. He was very businesslike and promised me forty percent of what he won. We were sitting at a counter at Schrafft's. I must have been crazy. Anyway, I finally decided it wouldn't be a bad investment. We went to my bank and I gave him five hundred dollars. There was a brightness about him and he seemed to have no doubts about anything. I liked that."

Charlie considered this, trying to imagine the young accountant being basically conned by the even younger Ackerman. "Did you make money?" Charlie asked.

79

Field laughed. It was a noise like wind in dry leaves. "He nearly lost it, did, in fact, lose most of it. The next morning I thought I'd been a terrible fool. I went to his room before work to demand my money back. He'd lost four hundred dollars the previous night and just smiled at me, said you had to give yourself room to lose. He even asked me for four hundred dollars more, but I thought he was crazy. He was crazy and I was crazy, too. I left and spent the rest of the day kicking myself. The next day, when I was sitting at my desk at work, he walked in. I worked at an insurance company at the time. He walked in past the secretaries, past everybody. I remember he was wearing an immaculate gray tweed suit and he looked like he could have been the son of the president of the company. Anyway, he walked up to my desk and put seven one-hundred-dollar bills down in front of me."

"What'd you do?" asked Charlie.

Field stopped rubbing and picking at his hands and sat staring at them. "I pushed the money back toward him and told him to 'let it ride.' He picked it up, put it back in his pocket, and walked out. After that we won and lost a lot of money together. Won mostly. Anybody who'd think I could kill him, well, that's crazy."

"If I keep looking for Lew's murderer and the police bother me about it, can I tell them that I'm following your instructions?"

"Are you a licensed private detective?"

Charlie had a sinking feeling. "No, I'm just a stable guard, but Lew was one of my best friends, too."

Field thought about this. Then he took a small, black box from his pocket, opened it and removed an ivory toothpick. Tentatively, he explored one of his upper molars.

"No," he said finally, "I can't help you. I don't want to get mixed up with it. Leave it to Peterson." He withdrew the toothpick, replaced it in the box and returned the box to his pocket. The box looked like a miniature coffin. "Anyway," he continued, "I don't think I'll be keeping the stable for long. With Lew dead I don't see much point in living here anymore."

"You'll sell the stable?"

"That's right. Dwyer might buy it."

"Isn't he a little old to be taking on new property?"

"His son-in-law would run it, Wayne Curry. Lew said he was a real hustler. He's been up here to talk to me a couple of times. You know him?"

"I've seen him around." The closest Charlie had ever gotten to Wayne Curry was one night when he and Lew had been having steaks at the Firehouse. Curry had come over to ask a question about some horse that Dwyer had claimed away from Ackerman at Aqueduct a few months before. What struck Charlie was that Curry hadn't bothered to apologize for interrupting and hadn't acknowledged Charlie's presence in any way. He had commented on this to Ackerman a few minutes later. Lew had shrugged and only said, "He's like that." Charlie tried to imagine him running Lorelei Stables.

"Look, Mr. Bradshaw," said Field, "I know you're upset about Lew's death, a lot of people are, but you can't just go racing off hoping to find the killer."

"I was a policeman for twenty years."

"And now you're a stable guard," said Field. "Let it go. Let Peterson do it." Field began rubbing the backs of his hands again. "After all, it's his job."

Five minutes later, Charlie was driving down Field's driveway. It was nearly dark and great rain clouds had begun to build up in the east. Turning onto Route 9p toward town, Charlie saw a blue Chevrolet parked along the side of the road. It was one of the police department's unmarked

81

cars and the man sitting at the wheel, Emmett Van Brunt, was a man Charlie had brought onto the force and worked closely with in the Community and Youth Relations Bureau. Charlie slowed and waved to him. Van Brunt looked the other way.

Charlie had felt disappointed by Field and since leaving his small office he'd been keeping his mind empty, just thinking about where he put his feet and getting into the car and manipulating it down the curving driveway. But then to be ignored by Van Brunt acted as a release for his feelings, and a current of anger swept through him. Almost without thought he slammed on the brake and pulled the Volkswagen over to the side of the road. He walked back to the blue Chevrolet and peered in through the window.

"Didn't you see me, Emmett?" asked Charlie.

Before Van Brunt could answer, a black Buick slowed, then turned into Field's driveway. It was being driven by a Saratoga policeman and Chief Peterson sat in the back seat. At that moment, Peterson was staring at Charlie and Van Brunt.

They watched the car disappear up the driveway, then Van Brunt said, "Shit, Charlie, am I going to get yelled at."

"Did Peterson tell you not to talk to me?"

Van Brunt began to roll up his window. He was a relatively young man with red curly hair and black horned-rimmed glasses. "Get out of here, Charlie. Go back to your fuckin horses."

A few big drops of rain began hitting the top of the blue Chevrolet. Charlie turned and walked back to his car.

Instead of driving in to Saratoga to meet Victor at the Backstretch, Charlie made a U-turn and headed home. It was raining hard by the time he got there. He ran to the cottage and began closing windows. Then he went to the back door and watched the rain make little pockmarks in the gray water until it got too dark to see. He turned back into the kitchen, took some eggs out of the refrigerator, and made a couple of fried egg sandwiches on soft white bread smeared with mayonnaise. As he carried them into the living room along with a beer, he could hear his wife's voice accusing him of eating trashy food, even though he had left her two years before. During the evening, he read about the outlaw empire of John A. Murrel in a book called *The Outlaw Years:* "My mother was of the pure grit: she learnt me and all her children to steal so soon as we could walk. At ten years old I was not a bad hand."

He was just getting into bed when the phone rang. It was Janet Macomb Claremon.

"Charlie? I'm sorry to bother you so late, but I've been thinking about Neal. There was one thing he said about two weeks ago, I don't know if it means anything. He never talked much and when he said this I guess he said it as much to himself as to me."

"What was it?" asked Charlie.

"He said something like, 'There's nothing worse than a stable fire.'"

"Is that all?"

"That's right. He said that and when I asked him what he was talking about, he wouldn't say any more."

11

"WHAT HE SAID was that Hyde Street was all dug up and you couldn't even walk down the sidewalk in some places. I then said they were fixin the sewer and he said that would do it and then I asked him if he was going to have any big winners this year and he said all his horses was going to be big winners and after that we didn't say much and a little after that I dropped him off. I mean, it wasn't a long ride or anything like that."

"So you figure he'd been over on Hyde Street?" asked Victor. He was talking to Wally Berrigan, the stooper who had driven Ackerman home from the Backstretch a week ago Tuesday. It was Thursday morning and they were sitting in Berrigan's room in a shabby rooming house on Phila. The walls were covered with an ancient yellow wallpaper with pink and violet peonies. A large framed photograph of a severe woman in black hung over the washstand. Berrigan had identified the woman as his mother, saying he took the picture with him to all the tracks in the country. Victor had said that was nice. Berrigan sat on the edge of the unmade bed, while Victor leaned back on a straight chair across the room by the window. It had stopped raining about half an hour before and now Victor could see that the emerging sun was making the sidewalks steam.

"I don't figure anything," said Berrigan. "I'm just telling you what he said." Berrigan was a puffy, sandy-haired man in his late forties and wore an undershirt, khaki pants, and a madras porkpie hat tilted back on his head.

"How far's Hyde Street from the Backstretch?" asked Victor.

"A coupla blocks. No more."

"He talk about anything else?"

"Nah, I mean, maybe he said it was a nice night and I agreed or maybe I was the one that said it was a nice night."

"Jesus," said Victor, "you'd make a pretty useless witness."

Berrigan stirred indignantly on the bed. "How'd I know he was going to go and get himself killed?"

"You gotta be prepared," said Victor. "A policeman or a detective, he's always gotta have his eyes open. Even when he's relaxing." Victor had been talking to Berrigan about ten minutes and felt he was beginning to scrape the bottom of this particular bucket. "What'd he seem like? I mean, neither of you said much and you both sat like lumps. Didn't you wonder what was goin through his head? You know, if they ask you these questions in a court of law, you'll have to be ready."

"I told you, he seemed upset like something was bothering him. And he was pretty, what do you call it, abrupt. Like he asked me for a ride home and I agreed and then he just sat there. I figured he had something on his mind so I pretty much left him alone. Maybe I asked him what he was doin in that neck of the woods and he said he'd some business to take care of."

"Business on Hyde Street?"

"Now that I can't tell you."

A few minutes later, Victor thanked Berrigan for his help, told him to keep his nose clean, and set off down Phila to the Executive to have a cup of coffee and a bagel. The morning had become warm and sunny and around him on the street were about a half dozen young women wearing various styles of shorts and halter tops. When Victor was feeling depressed and in need of a drink, halter tops were one of the things which convinced him that life wasn't so bad after all.

The man behind the counter at the Executive looked enough like Victor to be his son: the same heavy build, jowly face and hair that stood up as if electrically charged, although this man's hair was brown and he had more of it. His name was Dave.

He wiped the counter in front of Victor and gave him a glass of water. "You in here again, you old scoundrel? I better warn the waitress."

Victor sniffed the water, wrinkled his nose, and pushed it away. Then he did a little motion with his hips. "Yeah, well, they don't call me the beef torpedo for nothin," he said.

"Where's your buddy?" Charlie often came to the Executive to discuss the history of Murder Incorporated with this man's father.

"Out chasin crime, I guess. Gimme some coffee and a cinnamon bagel." It seemed to Victor that he too was out chasing crime but he wasn't sure where to begin. He asked himself what Charlie would do and after he thought about that for a while, he decided Charlie would first go over to Hyde Street and start knocking on doors to see if anyone had seen Ackerman that Tuesday night. It didn't seem very exciting, but maybe he'd find a lonely housewife.

Dave put the coffee and toasted bagel in front of Victor. "What kind of crime is Charlie chasing?" he asked.

"He's trying to find out who shot Ackerman."

"Now there's a guy I'd like to see fried," said Dave, pulling an imaginary switch in midair. "I liked Ackerman."

"Didn't we all," said Victor with his mouth half full of bagel. It had occurred to him he would need a photograph of Ackerman. Probably he could get one from the newspaper.

"Is Charlie working with Peterson on this?"

"Nah, Peterson's a dope," said Victor. "He couldn't even solve the kiddy crossword. Charlie's doin it by himself. 'Course I'm givin him some help."

When he had finished eating, Victor walked up Maple to the newspaper to get a photograph. Learning that he'd have to pay three dollars for it, he nearly refused, then changed his mind. The photograph, as well as the bagel, coffee, and maybe lunch, could go on an expense account and Charlie could reimburse him. The photograph showed Ackerman receiving a plaque at the Lions Club awards banquet the previous spring. Ackerman appeared so cheerful and in control of his world that it made Victor sad to look at it. Then he raised his hand and, like Dave at the Executive, pulled an imaginary switch.

Leaving the newspaper, Victor retrieved his car from a lot behind the Algonquin. He had an old rattletrap Dodge Dart that Charlie had found for him which was basically dark blue but also had large spots of gray primer. Actually, Victor was keeping his eyes open for a Volkswagen Beetle.

As he drove down Broadway and looked at the shops and Victorian buildings which seemed to glitter in the morning sun after a night of rain, Victor again congratulated himself for coming to Saratoga in April. Of course he wouldn't tell that to Charlie. No point in puffing him up. But Saratoga had been a helluva smarter choice than Chicago where he had nearly gone and then decided he simply couldn't face it. If what he didn't like was cities, then moving to Chicago wouldn't help, even though Victor's son Matthew lived in Chicago and worked at one of the hospitals as a medical technician, a job which to Victor seemed slightly less interesting than watching an ant cross a sidewalk.

Matthew and his wife owned a small house in Evanston and they had told Victor they'd fixed up the basement rec room for him. Victor could imagine the life, keeping his young granddaughter and grandson from killing each other, while Matthew and Bernice had a high old time. No, Chicago would have been the wrong choice and even though he liked Matthew he'd always thought of him as something of a sissy. As for Bernice, well fuck it, Victor would have had to kiss his girl-chasing days goodbye. Bernice thought two sexes were one too many and the world of hot pursuit was distasteful to her. Victor was all for broads getting a decent wage and being treated with respect, but that was no reason for him to unhook his genitalia and hide them up on the shelf along with the china figurines. Passing the Grand Union supermarket, Victor turned right onto Congress.

So at the last moment when his bags were packed and the ticket bought and Moshe howling in his wicker basket, he had called Charlie in desperation and Charlie had said come up to Saratoga. So he had, even though he hadn't seen Charlie for two years or even been in touch except for a couple of joking postcards asking him if he was keeping his clock clean and stuff like that. And Charlie had put him up on his couch for a couple of weeks even though he was allergic to cats and probably sneezed eighty zillion times a day. Then Charlie found him an apartment at the Algonquin and lent him money for this car and got him a job at the stable and well, shit, if he'd gone to Chicago, right now he'd probably be sitting in some clammy basement watching "Love of Life" while his grandkids tried to suck off his toes.

Hyde Street was two blocks long and lined with maples and oaks. Halfway up the block from Grand Avenue, Victor saw a yellow backhoe and some men in white hard hats working, presumably, on the sewer. Part of the road and sidewalk where he had parked seemed new and Victor guessed the crew was working its way down the entire street. He got out of the car, unlocked the trunk and removed a brown corduroy jacket which he shook several times, then put on over his gray sweat shirt. If he had thought about this earlier, he told himself, he would have neatened up. Well, it didn't matter. They could love him dirty, like it or not. There appeared to be thirty to forty older houses on Hyde Street, ranging from small to large. Taking a deep breath, Victor walked up to the first: a small, white house with white shutters. He knocked on the door.

After Victor knocked several more times, the door was opened by a nearly square man of his own age with a square head and big square hands and black unruly hair. The man wore workman's blue overalls and was holding a hammer. "I'm not buying," he said.

"That's okay," said Victor, "I'm not selling." He took Ackerman's photograph and held it up before the man's face. "You seen this guy around here a week ago Tuesday night?"

"Who wants to know?" said the man, not looking at the picture.

"I want to know. I'm Vic."

"Means nothing to me," said the man, beginning to close the door. From inside the house, Victor could hear laughter and applause from some television quiz show.

"Wait a second, Mac, this is a criminal investigation and if you don't answer with a simple yes or no, you could be in a helluva lot of hot water."

"You a cop?"

"Sorta."

"Where's your ID?"

"The kind of cop I am we don't have ID. I work with horses, you know, in security."

"You a horse cop?"

"No, I'm a stable guard."

The man made a grunting, coughing noise which Victor knew was meant as a humorous response, then he looked at the photograph. "That's Ackerman, isn't it? I recognize it from the paper. What makes you think he was around here?"

"I was just sort of wondering. You see him?"

"Nah, not me."

"Anyone in your house see him?"

"Nah, I live alone."

"That don't surprise me none," said Victor, turning away. Already he felt it was going to be a long day.

12

IT WAS A TALL, green metal gate with a twelve-foot
stone pillar on each side and the name "Dwyer" done in
metal letters over the top. It had been there as long as
Charlie could remember and he recalled bicycling by it
many times as a small boy. A chain link fence stretched
away in both directions. Charlie slowed his Volkswagen,
then drove through the gate. Before him he saw a parking
lot and beyond that some shed rows and a large house. To
his left a colt was being cantered around a training track.
The colt was gray with two white front feet, and it reminded
Charlie of the gray colt on which his mother was basing her
fortune.

That morning Charlie had received a card from his
mother mailed in Lexington, Kentucky, again urging him
to "bury the hatchet" with his cousins and stay out of trouble. She would be home in September. Ever Ready had apparently won again. On the reverse of the card was a picture
of the federal hospital for drug addicts in Lexington.

Hazel had purchased Ever Ready with her partner Hank
Justice, a free-lance electrician, at a claiming race in Saratoga for five thousand dollars. All four feet had been
bandaged and he had limped onto the track. Justice, however, had seen the same horse run in Louisiana two years

before and had seen it win. That time too the horse had been bandaged and limped, and later he learned that its trainer had spent a lot of time teaching it to limp to discourage bettors and increase the odds. He would also enter the horse in claiming races beneath its ability. Hazel happened to be with Justice that afternoon and the two claimed Ever Ready almost before he left the gate. Hazel had also bet one hundred dollars and when the horse won at fifteen to one, she believed she could see her dream motel slowly materializing through the fog. Now she and Justice drove around the Midwest in an old United Parcel Service truck with the horse sleeping on one side and them on the other. At sixty-three, she felt her life just beginning.

Charlie had been thinking of his mother a lot as he drove over to Dwyer's stable, since he knew that staying out of trouble was exactly what he wasn't doing. Last night he had almost decided once and for all to forget about Ackerman's death and let Peterson solve it his own way, if he was able. Then Janet Claremon's call had thrown him off again. Why should her husband talk about a fire? Then, that morning, as he watched the first sun break through the rain clouds over the lake, he decided he at least had to see Dwyer and find out why Claremon had quit or been fired or whatever had happened. He told himself he owed that to Lew; and as he went out to drink his coffee on his dock, he remembered mornings when the two of them had had breakfast on that dock and how beautiful it could be there.

Charlie parked his car next to a few others in a small lot and got out. Before him were two lines of green stables with piles of soiled straw at each end. A yellow feed truck had pulled up to the shed row which ran in front of the track. Charlie walked toward it. Nobody was around the truck, but nearby a young man was rubbing down a chestnut colt.

"Where can I find Dwyer?" Charlie asked.

"You got an appointment?"

"That's right. Is he around?"

The young man waved a hand over his shoulder. "He might be in the house. Curry's there at least."

Charlie started to walk in that direction, then paused. "You know a guy that worked here by the name of Neal Claremon?" he asked.

The man stopped rubbing the horse's front leg and glanced up. He wore dark glasses and Charlie couldn't see his eyes. "You'd better talk to Curry about that," he said.

At the end of the shed row was a two-story green house with a mansard roof and a large, screened-in front porch. Beyond it were two more rows of green stables. The four rows of stables nearly surrounded the house and approached to within twenty feet of it. In front of the house, near the track, was a small green barn, while beyond the house was a cluster of birches and a pond with a few ducks. Charlie climbed the front steps and opened the screen door.

"You looking for someone?"

Charlie peered into the relative dimness of the porch and saw a man lying on a chaise longue reading a newspaper. He recognized him as Dwyer's son-in-law, Wayne Curry.

"I'd like to talk to Mr. Dwyer," said Charlie.

"Does he know you're coming?" Curry got to his feet and walked toward Charlie. He wore khaki pants, a khaki shirt, and highly polished, brown jodhpur boots. Although a tall man, he moved quickly and delicately like a dancer. Charlie guessed he was about thirty. Curry carefully folded up the newspaper as he waited for an answer.

Charlie decided to avoid the question. "I'm Charles Bradshaw, chief of security at Lorelei Stables. We have a groom who was murdered this week and we found he had previously worked for Mr. Dwyer. I wanted to ask him some

93

questions." Charlie handed Curry his card. Curry looked at it briefly, folded it in half, drawing his thumb down along the crease, and stuck it in his shirt pocket.

"Who was killed?"

"Neal Claremon."

"Is it certain he was murdered?"

"He was shot in the back. Six times in the back."

Curry tossed his newspaper onto the chaise longue. "That's too bad. You're working with the police?"

"No, Chief Peterson is handling his own investigation."

"I'm not sure I understand what your jurisdiction is."

Before Charlie could make up an answer, the door of the house swung open and banged against the wall. Charlie looked to see Dwyer in his wheelchair at the top of a small ramp which led down to the porch. Slowly, Dwyer eased his chair through the door and down the ramp. Although it was a warm morning, he had a heavy red and blue plaid blanket over his legs and wore a beige Irish fisherman's sweater. Behind Dwyer, Charlie could see a walnut paneled room with photographs and paintings of horses on the wall and a glass bookcase filled with trophies.

"What's this about Claremon?" Dwyer asked.

"He's dead," said Curry.

Charlie was struck by the fact that Curry's face was not so much expressionless as constantly blank, like the face of a manikin. It was a tanned, almost ruddy face, narrow and smooth with a long thin nose and a narrow chin. His copper-colored hair was perfectly groomed: combed back over his ears and just brushing the collar of his khaki shirt.

"What happened to him?" asked Dwyer. His voice was low and breathy, and he spoke with effort.

"I found him yesterday at his cottage on Hedges Lake," said Charlie. "He'd been shot several days before."

"Who shot him?"

94

"The police don't know."

"How'd you happen to go out there?" asked Dwyer.

"He hadn't shown up for work for about five days and I wanted to find out why."

Dwyer glanced at his son-in-law. "But Claremon works for us."

"He quit about two weeks ago, Dad."

"You never told me that."

"I'm sure I did. I told you that night at the Firehouse. You said you didn't think we needed to hire anyone else."

Dwyer wrinkled his brow, then turned slowly from Curry back to Charlie. "Aren't you Charlie Bradshaw?" he asked.

"That's right."

"And so Claremon was working for Lew?"

"Lew hired him about ten days ago. I wanted to find out why he left here and came to our stable." Both Charlie and Dwyer looked at Curry who was lighting a cigarette.

"All he told me was he wanted to quit," said Curry, shaking out the match and dropping it in a glass ashtray on the table. "I figured he'd had a better offer someplace else."

"But he'd worked for us almost fifteen years," said Dwyer. "Why didn't he come to me? Did you offer him more money?"

Curry drew on the cigarette, then looked at Charlie and shook his head as if to indicate that wasn't how it happened. "I asked him why he was leaving, but he wouldn't say. As a matter of fact, his work had been getting a little sloppy and so when he said he wanted to leave I was just as glad."

Dwyer had seen Curry's gesture to Charlie and was growing red in the face. He had thick silver hair, blue eyes, and a large square jaw. He waited a moment before he spoke, allowing himself to calm down. "How was his work sloppy? He was one of my best grooms."

Curry held up one hand, then dropped it. "People

95

change," he said. Then he turned to Charlie. "Aren't you the guy who used to work for the police department and was fired?"

"I quit," said Charlie.

"Whatever," said Curry, "but I'm still not sure why you've come over here. Presumably the police will be talking to us. I don't see how you come into it."

Charlie had noticed that Curry's fingernails were perfectly groomed and shone slightly as if covered with clear polish. Glancing at Dwyer, he saw the older man was staring out at the training track. Charlie thought about how Curry had shaken his head and how Dwyer, though angered, had appeared to accept it. "We've a lot of expensive property coming into Lorelei," said Charlie, "a lot of new horses. First Lew is murdered, then Claremon. Whoever did it is still wandering around. It's my job to protect the stable so I'm trying to learn what's going on."

"You think the murders were connected?" asked Curry.

"Sure they're connected. Both men were killed with a silenced pistol and at this point nobody knows why."

Curry stubbed out his cigarette. "Isn't Chief Peterson working on it?" he asked.

"Peterson's prime interest is finding the murderer, while mine is to look out for the interests of Lorelei Stables. Perhaps I could talk to some of the other grooms and they could give me an idea why Claremon quit."

Curry folded his arms and glanced at his father-in-law, who was still staring out at the track. "Look, Mr. Bradshaw, I appreciate your concern and understand you have every reason to be worried, but I also feel I shouldn't let you talk to my men until I've talked to Peterson. Whatever your qualifications, he's the policeman and for all I know he may want to talk to my people first."

Charlie appeared to consider this, then said, "I don't see

how this would interfere with Peterson's line of inquiry. My concern is the security of Lorelei Stables."

"I appreciate that, but despite your connection with Lorelei you are still basically a private citizen and I can't allow you to wander around Dwyer Stables disrupting work just to satisfy your curiosity. Why don't we wait until Peterson comes here and I'll give you a call afterward. But I can't believe that Claremon's death had anything to do with Dwyer Stables and, although he left here abruptly, he also left on good terms."

Charlie knew he had been outmaneuvered. Looking at Curry's face, he still couldn't identify any expression, not even polite interest. It was like talking to someone who was wearing dark glasses. He began to think he had seen Curry someplace else in Saratoga, but he couldn't remember where. Charlie decided to try a different tack. "Do you have any ideas as to why someone might want to kill Ackerman and Claremon?"

Curry shook his head. "Lew Ackerman was a man I had a lot of respect for, but we all know he'd had a checkered past. I expect the solution to the puzzle will be found in something that happened ten, fifteen, twenty years ago. As for Claremon, if the two murders are really connected then possibly Claremon stumbled onto something and the murderer decided to kill him as well. What do you think, Dad?"

Dwyer, whose attention was still focused on the track, obviously hadn't been listening. He jerked his head toward Curry, looked blank for a moment, then said only, "I guess so." He hesitated, then turned toward Charlie. "I'd known Lew for twenty years and we fought and lied to each other and claimed each other's horses out from under our noses and spied on each other, but if I had one friend . . . ." Here he paused again. Up to this point, it had seemed to Charlie that Dwyer intended to give a speech, but now his voice changed and he began to speak more quietly. "I remember one time I sent a kid over to his stable to secretly clock one of his horses. Lew caught him and packed him into an old steamer trunk and shipped him back to me collect, but before he locked up the trunk he stuck in a bottle of Wild Turkey because he knew I liked it." He paused, then said, "You think Claremon's wife could use some money?"

"I expect so," said Charlie.

"I'll take care of it then." Dwyer had large red hands and he kept rubbing them back and forth on the arms of his wheelchair.

"I'll walk you back to your car, Mr. Bradshaw," said Curry.

Charlie was sorry not to talk longer to Dwyer, not necessarily about the murders but about Lew, to sit around and swap stories. He approached the wheelchair and stuck out his hand. "Thanks for your help, Mr. Dwyer."

Dwyer took it briefly and let it go. Charlie thought it was like holding a beanbag. "Good luck," said Dwyer.

Walking back along the shed row, Curry said, "My father-in-law is not a strong man, nor is he a happy man, and so I'm sorry you came and disturbed him."

Charlie didn't say anything. They walked past horses being rubbed down or washed, horses simply sticking their heads over the lower doors of their stalls. The green buildings were in need of paint and could use reshingling in places. Charlie was also struck by the fact that most of the people he saw were young, say, in their early twenties, and that they were all men. At Lorelei Stables at least half of the grooms were women. Curry walked a little ahead of Charlie, as if he were leading him.

When they reached the parking lot, Charlie said, "I like your father-in-law and I've got a lot of respect for him. And

I'm also sorry I upset him, if I did. On the other hand, I want to know why Claremon quit."

"As I suggested, perhaps he had a better offer."

Charlie watched a small, thin man lead a bay colt over to the hot-walker. "No," said Charlie, "Claremon went and asked Ackerman for a job. He didn't have one when he left here. Did he seem angry or frightened or bothered by anything?"

"All he said was that he wanted to leave. Maybe he did have some reason I don't know about. When Peterson comes, I'll suggest that he look into it."

"When Peterson comes."

"That's right."

Charlie looked up at Curry's face, trying to find some suggestion of what he was thinking. He guessed the man had spent some time in the service, because his face reminded Charlie of someone listening to a senior officer he didn't like: alert and withheld. Perhaps there was a trace of condescension. Charlie was tempted to tell Curry what Claremon had said about there being nothing worse than a stable fire, but he decided against it. Curry was too much of a question mark. As for Claremon, Charlie began to think more and more that the reason why he had left Dwyer's stable would also explain why he had been shot six times in the back.

13

CHARLIE PARKED his Volkswagen next to the phone booth and got out. To his left was the main box office of the Saratoga Performing Arts Center. The day had become hot and he paused to take off his tan suit coat and throw it in the back seat. About thirty people were lined up to buy tickets for the Philadelphia Orchestra, which would be giving concerts during the month of August. Beyond the gate was the open-sided, roofed amphitheater where Charlie had once taken his mother to hear Frank Sinatra. Behind him, bordering Route 52, stretched a parking lot which he guessed was about fifty acres. Charlie dug in his pocket for change and dialed Janet Claremon.

She answered on the fifth ring, sounding as if she had been asleep.

"How're you feeling?" asked Charlie.

"Better. Still sort of dazed. The police released the body to the funeral home. I guess he'll be buried this week. His brother's flying in from Salinas."

A groundkeeper on a red tractor mower passed close to where Charlie was standing and he had to strain to hear. "Is there anything I can get you or do for you?" he asked.

"No, I'll be okay in a few days."

100

"By the way," said Charlie, "do you know the names of any of the guys Neal worked with at Dwyer's?"

"I think so. Why do you want them?"

"I'm trying to get an idea why Neal quit. Maybe they'd know."

"Actually, I only know one man and he's not even working there anymore. He left about a month ago."

"Have any idea where he lives?"

"No, I don't, but last I knew he was working at the Citgo station across from the track. His name's Henry something-or-other and he's got bright red hair. If he's there, you won't miss him."

"Thanks, Janet."

The lawn tractor made another pass and when it had gone by Charlie heard Janet saying, "By the way, Charlie, the police were here again and Chief Peterson asked me not to talk to you. I thought you'd like to know."

Charlie felt touched by her complicity. "What did Peterson want?"

"He asked me if Neal gambled or was mixed up with any gamblers."

"You mean at the track?"

"No, I gather he meant cards and things like that."

Charlie thought about this. It indicated that Peterson was pursuing some line of inquiry which Charlie knew nothing about. He grew aware of Janet's slow breathing in the receiver and could almost visualize her in her bright, tidy kitchen with the photographs of New England villages. "What did you tell him?" he said at last.

"Nothing, I mean Neal never went out and hardly talked to anyone. And he never bet on horses unless he was pretty positive he had a sure thing."

"What did Peterson say to that?"

There was a pause, then with more spirit than she had shown so far, she said, "He said that maybe I was mistaken. Can you believe it?"

A little later, as he drove across Saratoga to see Henry at the Citgo station, Charlie knew he would soon have trouble with Peterson. He wondered if there were any way to placate him. It reminded Charlie of Canada Bill Jones who made several fortunes skinning greenhorns in three-card monte games on the Union Pacific during the 1860s and 1870s. When he became too well known and conductors kept throwing him off the trains, he wrote to the president of the company offering him ten thousand dollars plus an annual percentage of the take if he would grant Bill the sole franchise for three-card monte games on the Union Pacific. Bill further promised to bilk only Methodist ministers and travelers from Chicago, both of whom he hated.

The Citgo station was on a corner across from the main entrance to the track and across from the main stabling area and Oklahoma training track, which had been the original race track built by Old Smoke Morrissey in the 1860s. The elms and maples were particularly lush after last night's rain and as Charlie climbed from his car he paused to look at the bright green wineglass shapes rising above the white Victorian bandstand just inside the grounds. As he looked, it seemed that one delivery truck after another kept passing through the gates of the track from which came the banging of carpenters' hammers. Usually Charlie made a point of going on opening day. Last year he had been in Ackerman's box. This year he figured he would be with Victor standing somewhere along the rail, unless he could convince Doris to go.

Charlie walked toward the garage. In the back of one of the bays, he saw a tall, red-haired man changing a tire. "Are you Henry?" he called to him. The man straightened and dropped a flat metal bar that clanged on the cement.

"Who wants me?" he said. He had a soft Southern voice. Charlie guessed he was about six feet four and doubted he weighed 140 pounds. His red hair stood straight up on his head and Charlie guessed it felt bristly.

"My name's Charlie Bradshaw. I'd like to talk to you about Neal Claremon."

"Damn, weren't that awful," said Henry, "when I heard that on the radio, I figured it had to be the wrong Neal Claremon." He dragged a dirty red rag out of the back pocket of his blue coveralls, wiped his hands on it, and stuck out his right hand toward Charlie. "Henry Dietz," he said. "You a friend of Neal's?"

"I never met him, but he'd started working for Lorelei Stables and that's where I work as a guard." For some reason, Charlie didn't feel like dragging out one of his cards.

"So that's where he went, is it? He was lucky to get himself another stable job. That damn Curry, he fixed me so no other outfit will take me on."

"What do you mean?"

"Fired me for stealing a coupla watches, then refused to give me a reference. Shit, I'd worked for Dwyer eight years. What would I want to go and start stealing things for? You tell me that."

He looked so angry that Charlie wondered if he expected an answer. Dietz took out a pack of nonfilter Camels, offered one to Charlie, and when Charlie refused, lit one for himself with a shiny Zippo lighter that had the picture of a horse's head engraved on the side.

"You mean he accused you of stealing the watch just so he could fire you?"

"That's what I said, in't it? He tried to get me to quit by

103

giving me a hard time, making me take care of the worst horses, but I wouldn't have any of it. Old man Dwyer always gave me a square deal and I figured I'd stick by him."

"Why would Curry want to get rid of you?"

"He wants his own boys in there. For the past year or so, he's been dumping all the old hands. Me and Claremon was the last. Then, after I got fired at the end of June, I ran into Claremon and said he'd get it too. But he didn't think so. He said he'd talked to Dwyer and Dwyer said he'd keep him on no matter what. You see, it was Claremon that hauled Dwyer in after he'd had his stroke, and the doctor told him if he'd been out any longer, he'd of been a dead man for sure."

"When was this?" asked Charlie. The two men stood next to a white Volkswagen bus. Dietz was leaning against it with his arms folded and his cigarette dangling from his lower lip.

"Five years ago. We was at his farm in Kentucky. He and Claremon had ridden out somewhere checking spring foals. Then I remember I was rubbing down some horse and I looked up and here comes Claremon galloping across the field hollering. Dwyer was lying across his saddle and Claremon was sitting behind him. You know, Claremon was a fella who hardly ever said a word and to see him come galloping and shouting put the fear into you. Anyway, we rushed Dwyer to the hospital and called his daughter and Curry. They was living out in L.A. Then Dwyer has another stroke in the hospital and the doctor says he's not going to make it. He's a tough old bird though. He pulls through and's moving around before anyone figured he would, although he's changed a lot."

"How so?"

"Well, he's quieter, for one thing. He used to be a great shouter. Didn't mean much, like they say his bark was worse'n his bite. Then he was also the kind of fella that liked to do everything himself and once he gets out of the hospital he gets Curry to stay around and bit by bit Curry's doing more'n more stuff until by the time I get fired, Curry's running the whole show."

"Was the daughter around too?"

"Yeah, now and then, but she's got this interior decorating or design place out in L.A. so she never stays long. I guess Curry used to work there too, but he gave it up quick enough. She'd fly out every month or so and everything seemed hunky-dory, but I called it a pretty strange marriage."

"Does Dwyer have any other children?"

"Just that daughter. I heard he had a son that was killed in a car accident about twenty years ago but that was way before my time." Dietz ground the cigarette out on the heel of his boot. A red Fiat Spider with the top down pulled up to the pumps. "Scuse me a minute," said Dietz, walking toward it.

Charlie leaned against the VW bus and looked across East Avenue. Off to his left, he could see several exercise boys cantering horses around the Oklahoma track. He asked himself again why Claremon should quit Dwyer's only a short time after getting assurance that he wouldn't be fired. Maybe he really had been fired and Curry was lying. But Charlie doubted that. Claremon had told several people he quit and there seemed to be no reason to lie about it.

"What was Curry like to work for, as compared to Dwyer?" asked Charlie when Dietz had returned.

"He's a jumpy kinda guy. You never knew what he was going to do next. Also, he don't seem to like horses, like they make him angry or something. Dwyer might be tough on you, but you always figured he knew what he was doing. Not so with Curry. He wouldn't pay attention to feed orders

105

and getting new tack. There was always something going wrong. Then you never knew how he was going to act. One guy who'd been with Dwyer about ten years told him he didn't know what the hell he was doing and Curry hit him in the face. So help me, I was standing right there. Ignoramus, the guy called Curry an ignoramus and Curry hauled off and belted him. The funny thing was you couldn't even see it coming, like Curry didn't give any warning, just smashed the guy in the face and broke his nose. After that everyone gave Curry a lot of room. Then Curry starts hiring these new guys. For Christ's sake, some of them never even seen a horse before. I had to spend half my time showing them the ropes."

"What was Dwyer's reaction to this?"

"Nothing, he didn't say a word. I mean, I could of sworn he hated it, but he never said a word."

"Can you think of any reason why Claremon might have quit?"

"No reason, unless he'd had enough of Curry. Claremon was a strange guy. Did his work and never spoke. Now and then I'd take him out for a beer. We'd sit in a bar two, three hours and if I got ten words out of him about the weather I figured I was doing well." Dietz paused to light another Camel, then both men were silent as they watched a young woman in extremely tight white shorts and a tight white T-shirt ride by the gas station on a blue ten-speed.

"How'd you get framed for stealing the watch?" asked Charlie.

Dietz scratched his head, making his red hair stand up even more. "Well, there'd been a lot of petty theft going on, you know, watches and rings, maybe a wallet. I figured it was one of those new guys of Curry's. Then one day they had a search and found two watches in my bunk. Shit, I sure know I didn't put 'em there, but what could I do?"

106

"And you haven't been able to get another job?"

"No, I guess Curry talked to a bunch of other trainers."

"You go to Ackerman's?"

"Yeah, I talked to some guy, Warner his name was. He said they didn't need anyone."

"Would you rather work at a stable than work here?" asked Charlie.

"Mister, I been working with horses for twenty years, since I was sixteen. You think I want to be stuck here in a filling station?"

"Go see Warner again," said Charlie. "I'll talk to him. Mind you, I'm not promising anything because Warner doesn't like me much, but I'll give it a try."

Dietz looked momentarily suspicious. "Why do me the favor?"

Charlie shrugged. "Why not?"

After a second or two, Dietz began to grin. "Damn, I don't mean to be ungrateful. I'll shoot by there this afternoon."

"By the way," said Charlie, "when was the last time you saw Claremon?"

"Last Friday night, as a matter of fact, least I think it was him. I was in this bar around the corner, King's. It was pretty crowded. I saw Claremon and waved to him, but either he didn't see me or he ignored me. Personally I think he ignored me, 'cause by the time I got across the room to talk to him, he was gone. Just ducked out."

14

VICTOR DASHED up the steps, spun around, and raised the broken branch he held in his right hand. The chow dog which had chased him halfway down the block paused at the gate, panting. Victor thought its black tongue looked particularly mean-spirited. With a baleful glance, the dog turned and trotted back up the street. Victor threw the branch after it. The branch clattered on the sidewalk and bounced into the street. The dog didn't seem to notice. What the hell, thought Victor, those six houses he had missed because he had run past them as fast as a man could run, well, he could try them later.

Victor turned back to the door and rang the bell. As he waited, he straightened his jacket and checked his sweat shirt. It was almost dry. That had been another tactical error, along with calling the dog Fido. Afterward, Victor had realized that the woman was probably one of those rare creatures who are genuinely friendly to everyone. It had been wrong to assume she was making signals for him alone. And even if there had been such signals, it had been wrong to pinch her cheek while she was holding that pan of water.

Victor rang the bell again. There had been a name on the light post by the gate, but he had been running too fast to read it. The house was the last one on the block and bigger than the others: a three-story white Victorian house with gingerbread trim and a two-story carriage house in back.

A thin woman of about fifty in a black dress and white apron opened the door. "Maid," said Victor to himself. He held up a photograph of Ackerman. "Do you know if this man visited this house Tuesday before last," said Victor. "I'm conducting a survey."

"Survey?" asked the maid.

"That's right," said Victor, "I go from house to house asking questions."

Before the woman could respond, a man's voice behind her said, "Who is it, Lettie?"

"Some man with a survey, Mr. Dwyer."

She stood aside and in the hall Victor could see an old man in a wheelchair. He recognized the name Dwyer, knew that it belonged to someone connected with horses. For that matter, everyone he met seemed connected to horses. The man had on a brown suede jacket over a white shirt and his long white hair looked as if it had been just brushed. He had the sort of square jaw that Victor associated with cowboy heroes.

"What kind of survey?" asked Dwyer, rolling his chair up to the door.

Victor showed him the picture of Ackerman. "You know if this man was in the neighborhood a week ago Tuesday?" People in wheelchairs depressed Victor because they reminded him of the years his own wife had been confined to one. Even beyond that, this fellow looked decidedly down in the dumps. Victor hoped to be done here soon so he could return home to change. He had to be at work at five and it was four already.

"That's Lew," said Dwyer, surprised. He took the picture

109

and held it close to his face. "This is from the awards banquet last spring."

"That's right. Got it from the paper. Did you see Ackerman around here?"

"Lew was a friend of mine. Sure he was over here now and then."

"Yeah, but was he over here a week ago Tuesday? That's what I wanna know."

"What's this have to do with a survey?" asked Dwyer. He had a hoarse, gravelly voice which came, thought Victor, from a life of bossing people around.

"Nothin, that's just something I say to people to get their attention. Look, Mac, I'm sorry if Ackerman was a friend of yours. I liked him pretty much myself, but I gotta be at work in hardly any time at all, so maybe you could answer my question."

Dwyer rolled his wheelchair back several feet and looked at Victor in such a way as to make him think he'd been too frank. Then Dwyer looked away and rubbed his check roughly as if he were tired. In one hand, he still held the photograph which he had rolled up into a tube, making Victor afraid that he might damage it. "Why don't you come in and we can talk about this," said Dwyer.

Victor stood on the top step. Inside, next to Dwyer, was a large wooden coatrack and umbrella stand with a full-length mirror in which he could see Dwyer's reflection. "Thanks anyway," said Victor, "but as I say, I'm pretty rushed."

"Are you working with the police?" asked Dwyer.

"No, I'm Charlie Bradshaw's assistant at Lorelei Stables. We're tryin to clear this problem by ourselves. It's Mr. Bradshaw's opinion, and I must say I'm in agreement with him, that the police are pretty much being dopes about the whole thing. You mind givin me back that photograph before you mess it up?"

Dwyer seemed surprised to find he was still holding it. He handed it back to Victor. "Perhaps you could tell me what makes you think Lew was here that Tuesday night," he said.

"Not necessarily here," said Victor. "What my informants tell me is that Mr. Ackerman was someplace *around* here on that Tuesday night. He'd ditched his bodyguard, tellin him he had some business to take care of, then he came over to this street. I don't know, maybe he had some floozie. Now, it's 4:15, you mind tellin me if you saw him that night?"

"No, I didn't see him." Dwyer had a plaid blanket covering his legs and he began to pick at a loose strand of blue yarn. "You mean, you've been going up and down this street asking everyone these same questions?"

"That's right, except I missed a bunch of houses on account of a hostile dog. I hope to catch those tomorrow. You live here alone? I mean, is there anyone else he might of seen?"

"No, I'm sure he didn't come here. What does Bradshaw think Lew was doing that night?"

"He doesn't know. He's just trying to find out, thassall. Does someone live back there in that carriage house?"

"My son-in-law."

"Maybe Ackerman saw him. Is he around?"

Dwyer shook his head. "He's at my stable. Anyway, I'm sure Lew didn't see him."

Victor shrugged. "Maybe I can catch him some other time. You know anyone else around here that Ackerman might of seen?"

"Not offhand. Lew knew a lot of people. What makes you think he was on this street?"

"He mentioned to my informant how it was all dug up. So I figured he'd been along here someplace."

Dwyer rolled the wheelchair back a little. The hall floor was covered with a blue carpet and the movement of the chair was soundless. "Then it could have been the next street," said Dwyer. "It didn't have to be this street at all."

Victor sighed. He hated the thought of knocking on more doors. "I guess that's right," he said. "All I know is he was over in this area."

"Do you have any evidence to show that what he was doing over here had anything to do with his death?"

"Not really," said Victor, beginning to feel uncomfortable. "Just stands to reason, that's all."

"What reason? You mean coincidence?"

It occurred to Victor that he didn't know enough about Dwyer and his family to be able to do any more than antagonize the old man. Not that he minded antagonizing people, but Victor began to wonder if he was getting in over his head. "Look, Mr. Dwyer," Victor said, "I hate to cut this short, but I've got to get to work. I'll come back some other time to talk to your son."

"Son-in-law."

"That's what I said," said Victor.

15

BECAUSE OF THE HOSTILITY of his ex-wife and
the disapproval of his cousins, and because his ex-wife and
two of his three cousins had businesses on Broadway, Saratoga's main street, Charlie rarely went downtown or, if he
did, he stuck to Maple, a seedier street that ran parallel to
Broadway. But after seeing Henry Dietz and taking care of
some other errands, he decided to stop by the Montana
Bookstore to see if a book he had ordered on John Dillinger
had come in yet. He had to be at work at five and if the
book was in and the evening quiet, then he might get some
reading done if Victor would let him. Besides, he had about
twenty minutes to kill before driving to the stable and he
wanted to talk to Liz Hood, owner of the Montana and one
of the few non-ex-cons, non-track-affiliated, non-swimmers
who didn't feel themselves disgraced to be seen in Charlie's
presence.

He had parked his Volkswagen half a block away from
the Montana on Caroline and had almost reached the door
of the bookstore without seeing anyone he knew, when a
voice behind him called his name.

"Bradshaw!"

There was a certain stridency about the voice that made

Charlie wince. He turned to see Emmett Van Brunt looking embarrassed.

" 'Lo, Emmett, you decided to be friendly again?"

The plainclothesman scratched the back of his neck and glanced out at passing cars. "This is more official than that, Charlie."

Charlie smiled. "You here to arrest me then?" They stood in the middle of the sidewalk in front of the bookstore. People passed around them as if they formed a rock in a stream. In the front window of the bookstore a gray cat slept.

Van Brunt flushed and began to stutter, "It's like this, Ch-Charlie."

"Jesus, Emmett, you really did come to arrest me."

"No, no, Charlie. Peterson wants to talk to you, that's all. Don't make it so hard on me."

Charlie felt relieved. "Sure, I'll talk to him. I've got to be at work in about ten minutes. Tell him I'll stop by tomorrow morning. What time would be good?"

Again Van Brunt looked embarrassed. "It's gotta be now, Charlie." He had on black and white plaid trousers and a green and yellow plaid shirt, and the mismatched plaids made him difficult to look at, as if he were exemplifying nervousness or emotional tension.

"I've just told you, Emmett, I've got to be at work."

"That don't matter, Charlie."

"So you *are* arresting me. Emmett, why don't you just come out and say it?"

Van Brunt put his hands in his pockets and looked down at the sidewalk. "Not 'arresting,' Charlie, don't say 'arresting.' Peterson said he wanted a few words with you right away. Nobody's going to book you or anything like that."

"Great, that's just great. What if I said I couldn't do it

right now, would you use the handcuffs? Would I get charged with resisting arrest?"

"Jesus, Charlie!" Van Brunt looked around, hoping people hadn't heard. "Can't we just do this amicably? Why talk like a troublemaker?"

"Emmett, we worked together five years and now you're treating me like a crook. How friendly you expect me to be? All right, let's go. You won't need the cuffs."

Van Brunt's face brightened. "Thanks, Charlie. You'll see it's nothing. Just a little talk."

"I can imagine."

The police station was only another half block up Broadway, but in that distance Charlie saw several people he knew. A trainer beeped his horn at him. Jim Connor tooled by on a blue Kawasaki and gave him a thumbs up. He even saw his ex-wife's sister and business partner, who had married his middle cousin, Robert, who sold insurance and real estate. A few months before, Robert had offered Charlie a job in his office in order to get him away from the track, as he said. Charlie had refused. Lucy looked at Charlie from the steps of the Adirondack Trust across the street, looked at Van Brunt, then looked away, ignoring Charlie's wave as he entered the police station.

It had always struck Charlie as perverted that in a town full of racehorses, Chief Peterson should cover the walls of his office with pictures of Irish setters. Peterson raised them and they were the only creatures about which Charlie had ever heard him speak affectionately. He had now bred six champions, plus a good pack of also-rans. Along with colored pictures of his best dogs were framed pieces of parchment citing Peterson for improving the quality of the breed, whatever that meant. To Charlie it implied he had taught them to speak. Peterson leaned back in his black leather armchair and glared at Charlie as he entered.

"You know, Charlie, far as I can see it, you're only makin trouble for one fuckin person."

"How's that, Chief?" Charlie sat down in the smaller black leather armchair on the other side of the half-acre desk. He was irritated at being dragged off the street and saw no reason to be placating. Van Brunt still hovered in the doorway. Peterson snapped his fingers at him and Van Brunt disappeared. It was a gesture, Charlie knew, held over from Peterson's years with the military police, and seeing it Charlie once more patted himself on the back for having brains enough to quit the police department.

"Tell me, Charlie," said Peterson, "why is it that wherever I go, I find you been there first muddying the water?"

"What do you mean, Chief?"

"Don't play dumb with me. Yesterday, out at Claremon's, I believed you when you said you'd gone there to see why he hadn't shown up for work. But then I find you've gone back and been bothering Mrs. Claremon with questions, then you go bother Field. Then I start hearing wherever I go in Saratoga that you're going to solve my case for me, that you don't think I got the brains to do it myself. How you think that's goin to make me feel, Charlie?"

Charlie wasn't sure if Peterson was serious. "I never told people I was going to solve any case."

"Oh, yeah? I go into the Executive for a sandwich and the guy behind the counter tells me how he hears I can retire because Sherlock Holmes Bradshaw is on the trail. Then I hear it from grooms and bartenders, bums in the drunk tank. Look, Charlie, I got fuckin feelings like anyone else. Then I come back here and I find you been bothering old man Dwyer. I don't like that, Charlie. Dwyer's a personal friend of mine. What'd you want to go over there and bother him with questions for? His health's not good and maybe his mind's a little iffy besides."

"Did he call and complain?" asked Charlie.

Peterson raised his thick eyebrows as if to indicate that of all the dummies he knew Charlie took the cake. He got up from his desk, walked around it, and stood in front of Charlie, bouncing on his toes. He wore his three-piece blue suit with a silver chain across his stomach, and as Peterson bounced the silver chain did small leaps.

"Charlie," said Peterson, "can't you get it through your head that you're not a cop? How can I talk to these people when you've already been at them? It's none of your business, can't you see that? What am I going to do, lock you up?"

Charlie leaned back in his chair and tried not to look at Peterson. Not only did he not like the Irish setters, he also disliked their silly robot postures, and he wondered how much you had to pound on a dog's head to make it stand like that.

"Look, Peterson, I know you're doing a job. Well, I'm doing one too. Lew Ackerman hired me to protect Lorelei Stables and that's what I'm doing. I'm not trying to interfere with you, I'm just trying to make sure nothing else happens." As he said this, Charlie wondered if he believed it. He supposed he did, although it didn't indicate his anger at the murderer or his lack of faith in Peterson.

"I asked Field if you were working for him and he said no."

"Field's an accountant. I'm working for Ackerman."

"He's dead."

"I can't help that." It occurred to Charlie that he had never spoken to Peterson so aggressively before.

"Charlie, you can't think we're sitting still on this. We got leads and we're going after them."

"You mean Field?"

"Field schmield, I'm not ruling him out, but right now he's back on the shelf. No, everything we've learned points to bigger fish than Field."

"Tell me about it."

"No can do, Charlie."

"You think it's tied into gambling, right? Lew was pretty dead set against gambling. Is there any connection there?"

Peterson squinted his eyes at Charlie, then stepped back and sat down on the edge of his desk, nearly knocking over a brass nameplate that said, "Harvey L. Peterson—Commissioner of Public Safety." "Maybe the gambling's part of it," he said. "As you know, there's a move on to start gambling again in Saratoga. Some people figure what works in Atlantic City can work twice as well here. As you say, Ackerman was dead set against it. He knew the guys who were pushin to open the casinos and thought they'd bring nothing but trouble. You know, a number of people in Albany would like to see gambling up here. It'd mean a lotta new tax dollars. Ackerman's been down in Albany trying to line up the people who are against any reopening. It made him unpopular and there was some big money on Long Island that wanted him out of the way."

Charlie thought about this. It had been twenty-six years since the casinos had closed following Senator Kefauver's evidence that they were run by a syndicate of racketeers. Governor Dewey had called for a special grand jury and that had been that. The next year the biggest of the great hotels, the Grand Union, had closed its doors for good, putting Charlie's mother out of a job. The first casino had been opened in 1842 by Ben Scribner and during the next 110 years gambling had been banned several times by reform-minded citizens. Charlie knew there was a movement to reestablish gambling in Saratoga and that Ackerman had been against it. He had also assumed that like it or not gambling would some day be legalized, if only because Saratoga was that kind of town.

"What about Claremon?" asked Charlie.

Peterson got up and walked over to a color photograph on the side wall showing a particularly silly looking Irish setter sniffing the wind in a corn field. With his thumb, Peterson moved the picture to the right, then left. It hadn't seemed to Charlie that the picture had ever been crooked.

"You were right about that," said Peterson. "Ballistics showed they were killed by the same .9mm handgun. What I figure is that Ackerman told Claremon something or Claremon overheard something that made him dangerous to the murderer."

"Maybe it was the other way around."

"What d'you mean?" Peterson walked back to his desk and sat down.

"Maybe Claremon told Ackerman something."

"What could a guy like that tell anybody?"

"Why did he leave Dwyer's stable?"

"Grooms, how can you figure them? He left, that's all. I mean, I think Wayne Curry's doing a heck of a job over there, but you don't need to tell me that his ways are going to be different from the old man's. You go into a place, you gotta have people who are loyal to you. Claremon sounded like quite an eccentric guy. Maybe he and Curry bumped up against each other too much and so finally Claremon quit."

"Is that what Curry told you?"

"I'm telling you, Charlie, Curry's all right."

"Did you talk to any of the people who worked with Claremon?"

"Some of them. They couldn't tell me anything I didn't already know. Jesus, Charlie, I'm trying to explain to you, that's a blind alley."

"What makes you think so?"

Peterson stretched his arms out before him on the desk and clasped his hands. It made him look avuncular and, Charlie thought, somewhat patronizing. "Look at the way Ackerman and Claremon were killed. That wasn't any amateur job. It all points to some racketeer shooting. There're a lotta good men working on this case and all the feedback points to gambling interests. Why'n't you take a rest? I know you're worried about the stable, but there's nothin you can do up here. Bullying old men and telling everyone in town what a great cop you are, believe me, Charlie, that's no way to get your old job back."

16

VICTOR'S GRATITUDE to Charlie for hiring him as a guard was tempered by the knowledge that the other four guards were all ex-cons. Stumble bums, Victor called them, although they weren't bums and didn't stumble. He even liked them. That, however, was Victor's own secret, since he believed his fellowman was better off with hostility than friendship. It kept people on their toes.

The guard that Victor liked best was Rico Medioli who had been born and raised in the same part of lower Manhattan as Victor himself. Although only twenty-four, Rico had spent six years in jails and juvenile homes, having been first sent away at age twelve for breaking and entering. The sentencing had come after fifteen or seventeen arrests, Rico couldn't remember for sure. He remembered his first arrest at age eight for shoplifting and his last at twenty-one for breaking into a wealthy Upper West Side New York apartment, but in between was such a confusion of being tossed into and booted out of the slammer, as he called it, that the specific details were lost.

When Rico had been released from Auburn six months before, he decided to go straight—not because of a newly defined sense of right and wrong, but because he decided there was nothing more boring than criminal life as experienced behind bars. When he had gotten out of jail, he told his probation officer he didn't want to return to New York City, a place of many temptations, and the probation officer sent him to Charlie.

What Victor liked about Rico Medioli, apart from the qualities of a personality hardened by prison, was that he obviously had a bowling ball in his recent ancestry. He was short and square with a thick neck, weight lifter's shoulders, and very curly brown hair. He looked, Victor thought, as if he had once been eight feet tall, then had a heavy weight fall on his head, reducing him to about five feet five. He looked as if he had been designed to roll rather than walk.

It always cheered Victor to see him and so when Rico and Jack Krause strolled into Charlie's small office next to the tack room shortly after midnight, Victor felt his lot measurably improved. Not that he found Charlie bad company, but Charlie was being sullen about something and had spent the entire evening reading some book about John Dillinger. To make matters worse, it was raining again and Victor's feet were wet from making his rounds along the shed rows, plus his legs were tired from spending the day wandering up and down Hyde Street.

"Whatcha doin here early, you no account sneak thief, you aren't due for an hour yet?" Victor winked at Krause who shook his head.

"Thought I might catch you poundin your pud or dorkin that she-goat they're keepin with Best-in-the-West."

"I was tempted," said Victor, "but I saw she still had your ring hanging from her scrawny neck. You and Krause keepin company these days? Least you can't knock him up."

"Nah, I ran into him at the Backstretch and he told me how Charlie is showin the cops what for, so I decided to pop by and find out about it."

Regretfully, Charlie put down his book. He had reached

the part where Baby Face Nelson had leaped for his machine gun to polish off Homer Van Meter in Nelson's hotel room in St. Paul. Van Meter had laughed at Nelson's cavalry charge bank holdup tactics and was barely saved by Dillinger who assured Nelson they were "all pals here."

"I'm not showing the police anything," said Charlie. "I've done as much as I can do."

Charlie, Victor, and Rico were all wearing gray guards' uniforms with the name Lorelei stitched in red on the left breast pocket. Krause, in a brown suit, was in the process of shaking out his raincoat and hanging it on a hook behind the door. There had been thunderstorms off and on all evening and Krause and Rico had caught the tail end of one as they ran from the parking lot to the stable.

"He's fuckin scared of them," said Victor. "Fuckin chief of police yanked him in this afternoon and threatened to throw his ass in jail. When I first met Charlie, he had the whole New York City police department chasing after him. Think that bothered him any? Not fuckin likely. He went down to the Apple to do something and he did it, cops or no cops."

Charlie shook his head. It made him uncomfortable to be the butt of snappy conversation. "I went down there to help somebody and he wound up getting shot and thrown in jail."

"Yeah, but he deserved it," said Victor. "Least the girl got off. What happened to her anyway?"

"Her parents took her to Europe."

"Personally," said Victor, "I'd rather go to jail than go to Europe. Least in jail you can drink the water."

"Is that the girl that cost you your job and made your wife dump you?" asked Rico. He stood in the center of the room and had begun touching his toes, moving quickly and easily, giving the floor a rap with his knuckles each time

123

he bent. He was someone, Charlie thought, who morally disapproved of standing still.

"Don't you believe it," said Victor. "Fuckin Charlie, he's like the driven snow, didn't even lay a finger on her. Chance missed is life lost, that's what I always say."

"Charlie, what do you mean you've done as much as you can do?" asked Krause. He had taken a chair by the door and was wiping splashes of mud off his pants with a paper towel.

"Just what I said. I thought I had some information, but it turned out to be nothing. Not only that, but I was interfering with Peterson, I mean, interfering to no purpose."

"But even if you did a little bit," said Krause, "that'd be more'n what Peterson's doing."

"That's not true. Peterson's following some pretty good leads. All I'm doing is making things difficult for him."

"Let's just say," said Rico, "that you kept pushing along on your own. What would you do that Peterson's not doing?"

Charlie considered this. He was leaning back in his swivel chair and had his feet up on the desk. Victor sat across the room in a ragged brown armchair. The room was in one corner of a barn and the walls were whitewashed pine boards. On the wall behind Charlie was a poster showing Pancho Villa mounted on a horse over the words "Viva la Revolución."

"I guess," said Charlie, "I'd spend some time looking into Dwyer's stable."

"Lew and Dwyer were pretty close friends," said Krause. "Didn't Dwyer give the eulogy at the cemetery?"

"That's true," said Charlie, "but something doesn't feel right over there. For a stable only four days before a meet, that place looks half empty."

"Dwyer's an old man," said Krause. "Maybe he just

124

wants to slow down a little."

"Yeah, but he ain't the guy runnin the place," said Victor. "He's turned the whole shebang over to his son-in-law, Wayne Curry."

"Never met the man," said Krause. "Seen him of course, but never met him."

"He's been workin down at Dwyer's farm in Kentucky for about four years," said Victor. "Just came up here last September."

Charlie looked at his friend who had paused to put his fingers in his mouth and check on a tooth to see if it wiggled. "How do you know that?" Charlie asked.

"Common knowledge," said Victor.

Krause leaned forward and put his elbows on his knees, letting his big hands hang loosely before him. Although he wore nothing but dark suits, they always looked wrong on him, as if he were in disguise. "I drove Lew to the wedding," he said, "but I waited in the car while he went in. I'm not much of a one for churches. That must of been in '72 or '73."

" '72," said Victor.

"I guess so," said Krause. "Lew said Dwyer was just as glad to see her married. You ever run into her when she was at Skidmore, Charlie? She had that old white Caddie convertible. Had a pretty heavy foot."

Since seeing Dwyer that morning, Charlie had been trying to remember the daughter. With the mention of the white Cadillac convertible, he began to recall a thin girl with long blond hair who drove too fast. He didn't in fact remember much more than that; but there was a period of a few years where it seemed that whenever he was sent to investigate a loud party or kids being rowdy out at the lake, there had been this blond girl in her white Caddy convertible.

"I'd forgotten," said Charlie. "She lost her license and

we picked her up a couple of times driving without it. Then about ten years ago she left town."

"Went out to Los Angeles," said Victor. "She's a decorator or designer or somethin out there. Met Curry down at Belmont when she came back on a visit. You know the story, whirlwind romance."

"Where'd you hear all this?" asked Charlie.

Victor laid one finger along the side of his pear-shaped nose. Each side was decorated with little nets of red capillaries. "I knows what I knows," he said. He got to his feet and took Charlie's yellow slicker from a hook behind the door. "Mind if I wear this? I gotta check the horsies." He pulled on the yellow slicker and stuck the yellow rain hat on the back of his head. "Don't tell any dirty stories without me," he said.

"Check on Red Fox, will you, Vic? He doesn't like thunder."

"Him and me both. Hey, Rico, were there many other cars in the lot when you came in?"

"Just a couple. Why?" Rico had stopped touching his toes but was still standing in the middle of the room looking ready.

"No reason. Lotta the guys went to the movies to see *Snow White*. I wondered if they were back yet." Victor opened the door and Charlie could see it was still raining heavily. "I hate soggy feet," said Victor and disappeared.

Krause took a thick cigar from the inside pocket of his jacket, tore off the cellophane, and sniffed it appreciatively. Charlie hated cigar smoke, but feeling that Krause had been more upset by Lew's murder than anybody and was thus in greater need of comfort, he remained silent through the ritual of snipping off the tip of the cigar with some silver pocket tool, then lighting it with a fat kitchen match.

"I don't like to see you giving up on the investigation,

126

Charlie," said Krause, through a cloud of smoke. "I told you I'd pay you. Any trouble you get into, I'll see you get out."

"I appreciate that, Jack, but it won't work. I asked Field if he'd back me, but like he said, I'm just a stable guard. If I keep going against Peterson, I'll get me and the stable in trouble. Besides, Peterson's got a police department of nearly eighty men and has access to every other department in the country. I can't just poke around."

"Tell him to kiss your ass," said Rico. "You got your own police department. There's Krause and you got five eager guards. What more'n you need than that?"

Charlie laughed. "Like I said, let's give Peterson more of a chance."

"Let's say, just for the sake of argument," said Rico, "that you kept up with your investigation, what would you do next?"

"I told you, I'm not doing any more." Charlie picked up his book on Dillinger.

Rico put his hands on his hips and violently began twisting his torso from left to right. "Yeah, but let's say you did," he asked, "what would you do next? You can answer me that, can't you?"

Charlie put his book back down. He'd be leaving in half an hour and could read at home. "I'd find out more about Wayne Curry," he said.

Victor kept his head bent as he followed the circle of light thrown on the mud and wet grass by the flashlight in his hand. Even though rain was running down his face and neck, and even though his shoes had become small buckets, he was chuckling to himself. After seeing Dwyer that afternoon, he had stopped by the Backstretch and had gotten a lot of useful information about Dwyer, his daughter, and her husband from Doris and the owner, Berney McQuilkin. He wasn't sure what he'd do with it and he didn't intend to do anything until he had checked the houses he had missed on Hyde Street. But more and more Victor began to suspect that Ackerman had visited Dwyer's house that Tuesday night. Who he had seen or why he had gone, Victor didn't know, but the possibility of Ackerman seeing one of Dwyer's neighbors for something completely unconnected to Dwyer seemed improbable.

But he had enjoyed seeing Charlie's surprise as he had trotted out bits of information about Dwyer's daughter, and as he walked along the shed row he indulged in a fantasy in which he went ahead and solved the case by himself, perhaps concluding with one of those classic scenes where he brought together all suspects and interested parties and bit by bit unfolded to them the story of the crime as the actual murderer grew increasingly nervous and at last made a bolt for the door. How would he stop him? He imagined Moshe, his one-eyed cat, grown huge and carrying the murderer back into the room as he had once seen him carry a rat: almost tenderly between his jaws. And who was the murderer? That, unfortunately, he couldn't tell.

As he approached Red Fox's stall, he was jarred from his thoughts by seeing that instead of being closed, the Dutch door was wide open, bottom and top. Victor hurried toward the door, his flashlight projecting a bobbing circle of light on the muddy ground and white and green stalls. Running into the stall, he saw immediately that Red Fox was gone. Then, just as quickly, he sensed a movement behind him, but as he began to turn someone grabbed him, wrapping his arms around Victor's shoulders, and pinning Victor's arms to his sides. Victor kicked backward and heard a grunt, but before he could do more a second person took hold of his left hand, knocking the flashlight into the straw. There followed a brief struggle as Victor tried to pull his hand free and the man behind him tightened his bear hug. Victor could hear the man breathing in his ear, but then his attention shifted as in the dim light he saw the man before him raise his hand above his head. Victor threw himself back, trying to yank his arm free. Then the man violently swung down his arm and a length of pipe smashed down onto Victor's left arm between the wrist and elbow.

It seemed to Victor that his whole arm had been jabbed with pieces of glass and he opened his mouth to scream. But before he could do more than suck in his breath, there was another quick movement and something hit him hard in the stomach. Simultaneously, the person behind him let go and shoved him forward. Victor staggered across the straw, retching and holding his stomach with his good hand. The flashlight between his feet made his shoes look big and muddy. Then he sensed another movement and as he tried to stagger away he was hit on the head. Again, the pain was like being stabbed with glass. As he fell, he tried to catch himself with his damaged arm and as the arm buckled beneath him Victor screamed a high scream like a car suddenly braking or wind rushing through a crack in a door. He fell on his side and held his arm to his chest. It felt as if his body was scattered in a dozen pieces around the stall. Trying to focus on his surroundings, he realized he was alone. He told himself he had to get Charlie and the last thing he remembered was crawling toward the door and feeling the rain spatter against his face as he crawled out of the stall.

When he awoke, he was being lifted out the back door of an ambulance. Looking up, he saw Charlie's worried,

129

round face looking down from one side of the stretcher and Krause looking down from the other. The pain in his arm was such that he felt sure he would pass out again.

"Somebody fuckin whopped me, Charlie. They steal Red Fox?"

"No, he was out on the track. He'll be okay. You see anybody?"

Victor shook his head. He felt he was going to be sick. The ambulance attendants wheeled him through the emergency entrance into a brightly lit hallway. A doctor and two nurses hurried toward him. "Didn't see a fuckin soul," he said.

An hour later, Victor, wearing a blue hospital gown, was settled into a private room where he was to spend the night. For observation, as he had been told. His left arm had been broken and was now in a cast. Charlie and Krause had gone with him up to the room, along with a little orderly who knew Charlie and who brought in extra pillows, magazines, and a triple shot of Jack Daniel's in a paper cup. He was a thin little man, not much taller than five feet, and was one of those unfortunates who don't go bald in a smooth process but in bits and pieces, making his hair look like something that the cats had fought over.

As Victor began to sip the Jack Daniel's, Charlie sat down on a chair next to the bed. He had had no chance to talk to Victor since his friend had been admitted. "So you have no idea who broke your arm?" asked Charlie.

"None. Couldn't see their faces. Couldn't even see what they were wearin except it was dark. Shit, it could of been a coupla broads. What'd I get hit with?"

"I found a length of lead pipe in the straw," said Charlie. "The police must have it by now."

Charlie had seen the police arriving just as he had been leaving in the ambulance. Rico had shown them around

130

and presumably they would soon appear at the hospital. Charlie had telephoned Rico and learned that the police suspected what Charlie had at first suspected himself, that is, that Victor had accidentally interrupted two men who had been trying to do something to Red Fox. That was what Charlie had originally thought, but now he wasn't so sure. There was no evidence they had tried to steal Red Fox and there was no evidence he had been physically tampered with. Of course that couldn't be certain until the horse was examined by the vet, but the groom, Petey Gomez, had checked him over pretty carefully and Red Fox had seemed fine, according to Rico.

Beyond that, what struck Charlie was that Victor's arm had been broken, well, carefully. As if the intruders had come for the sole purpose of breaking the arm. The problem, however, was that Charlie knew no reason why anyone should want to hurt Victor. The only thing he could think of was that since Victor had been wearing Charlie's yellow raincoat, they had attacked him mistakenly. As he thought this, Charlie wondered what reason anyone had for hurting him, and with the question came the realization that it had to have something to do with Ackerman's death. Sitting next to Victor's bed and watching him sip the Jack Daniel's, Charlie tried to guess the odds of convincing Peterson that he himself had been the intended victim. He knew, however, that the police chief would instead believe the simpler interpretation, that is, that Victor had been attacked because he had interrupted somebody tampering with Red Fox.

The small man with the patchwork hair appeared at the foot of Victor's bed. "Is there anything else you would like, Mr. Plotz, a sandwich or maybe a deck of cards? I can get you a *Playboy*."

"Nah, that's all right. Thanks for the drink."

131

After the man left, Victor asked Charlie: "He a friend of yours?"

"Sort of. He was one of the first guys I ever arrested and I stayed in touch with him in prison. Got him a lot of books about birds, if I remember right."

"What was he in for?"

"Killed someone in a bar."

"How come?" Victor tried to sit up, then winced and stayed where he was.

"I don't know, he said the man had stolen his wife's affections. Something like that. I sort of doubted his wife had ever cared much for him in the first place. Nice guy though, once you got to know him."

Victor drank off his Jack Daniel's and dropped his cup on the floor. "Jesus, Charlie, I should of known that hangin around somebody who only knows criminals and reprobates would land me just where I am right now. I must be the only fuckin respectable friend you have."

"That's probably true," said Charlie.

17

CHARLIE ALWAYS DID his best thinking underwater. As he negotiated a slow turn at the end of the pool, then started back for his second length, he felt his body beginning to free itself from the cocoon of frustration and social convention which had confined his day. It was about quarter past seven Friday evening and around Charlie in the YMCA pool were seven or eight other swimmers engaged in the slow process of accumulating laps.

Charlie liked that. He liked the comradely anonymity of the pool. He liked that for the most part the people around him knew him primarily as a swimmer: someone who could be counted on to do a certain number of laps and stay in his own lane.

Jim Connor swam on one side of him, much faster and more graceful, but still a friendly presence. On the other side was a young woman in a dark blue Speedo suit. Outside the pool, she was chunky and heavyset, but in the pool she was completely streamlined, like a large beautiful seal. Charlie saw himself a little like that: not beautiful exactly, but streamlined and efficient, moving purposefully in the one place in life where he didn't stumble over his feet.

In the eyes of his family, he knew he had begun to stumble badly. That morning he had received a telephone call from James, his oldest cousin, five years older and the owner of a small construction company. He had said Chief Peterson had dropped by to tell him Charlie was acting foolishly and irresponsibly, interfering with a criminal investigation to the extent the criminals were most likely benefiting from his intrusion. James didn't want to interfere, didn't want to tell Charlie what he should or should not do. Far be it from him to remind his young cousin the family had a position to maintain in the community, but perhaps Charlie wouldn't mind dropping by the office that afternoon and they could have a chat over a cup of coffee.

The call had come at 7:30 that morning, waking Charlie after three hours sleep. It was James's contention that a mentally, emotionally, and physically healthy person only required four hours sleep per night, and he proved this by never sleeping more than four hours himself. It was this feat, he believed, which was also responsible for his business success, his election as president of the Lions Club, and his being a six-time recipient of the Little League Booster Award. He also believed, somewhat inaccurately, that Charlie required vast quantities of time-squandering sleep and that he had inherited this weakness from his father's side of the family. Charlie had expected James to remind him once again how his father had welched on his IOU's to bookies by sending a bullet through his brain, but James had chosen to be subtle. In any case, Charlie had not gone to his office and had no intention of going.

As he swam back and forth, he grew increasingly certain that the attack on Victor had been intended for himself and, further, the attack was an indication that his small investigation was seen by someone as a threat. The veterinarian's report on Red Fox showed the horse had not been tampered with beyond being freed from his stall. Chief Peterson at first argued that Victor had interrupted the tampering, but it now seemed clear Red Fox had escaped to the training track about ten minutes before Victor had appeared on the scene. Beyond this, Charlie was not happy that it had been Victor who was attacked, rather than himself, since it gave Charlie the nagging sense there was information unaccounted for. The fact Victor was wearing Charlie's yellow slicker seemed to explain this, but still Charlie wondered if something wasn't being left out.

In any case, Peterson had finally agreed that the purpose of the intrusion was most likely the attack rather than the horse. Victor hadn't simply been knocked unconscious, his arm had been neatly and carefully broken. But although Peterson had come to this conclusion, the reasons he gave for it were different than Charlie's.

Charlie had stopped by police headquarters that morning to see if Peterson had any new information about what had happened. Peterson was even more patronizing than usual. "Now, Charlie," he had said, "you know and I know that Plotz has a bad habit of chasing the women. What I figure is that some husband or some boyfriend finally had enough. Who can blame them, an old guy like that?"

"Maybe they were after me," Charlie had said.

"How come? You after the women, too?"

"Perhaps I've upset someone by asking questions about Ackerman."

"Aw, Charlie, give me a break. I already told you what I thought about the case. You know as well as I do that when Plotz likes some female, he just asks them point-blank and when they say no, he just keeps asking them. Some guys don't like that and I can't say I blame them."

Charlie had spent some time arguing with Peterson, but the police chief just shook his head and looked wise. The result was that Charlie, who had sincerely decided to give up investigating Lew Ackerman's death, decided to press his investigation a little further.

The girl in the blue tank suit had left the pool to be replaced by a man in his mid-seventies whose free style stroke was a combination of the dog paddle and drowning. It seemed to Charlie that if even the smallest bird landed on this swimmer's shoulders he would certainly go under. Charlie recognized him as an ex-city councilman whose suspect real estate deals allowed him to make a fortune when the Interstate was put through at the edge of town. Beyond that, Charlie recalled a questionable interest in little girls. In the lane next to Charlie, however, he was just a man doing his laps.

As a consequence of Peterson's dismissal of the attack on Victor, Charlie had returned to the stable around noon to assemble what Rico Medioli called Charlie's Police Force. Besides Victor, who stayed home, and Krause and Rico himself, there were: Phil Tyler, an ex-real estate and confidence swindler who had sold thousands of acres of phony property in Florida, New Mexico, and Arizona and whom Charlie had hired primarily because he looked like the White Knight in *Alice Through the Looking Glass;* John Wanamaker, slightly younger than Charlie, ex-burglar and drunk and now a born-again Christian and member of A.A. who never did his rounds without his Bible; Eddie Gillespie, a none-too-bright youngster from nearby Ballston Spa who was only happy at speeds over 100-miles-per-hour and was presently on probation for car theft. As these five men gathered in Charlie's office, he realized they were some of the people he liked best in Saratoga.

Charlie explained what he knew about the two murders, said what Peterson's ideas were, and went on to say that he felt they should learn more about Dwyer's stable and Wayne

136

Curry in particular. He didn't necessarily suspect Curry, but there were unanswered questions arising from Neal Claremon's departure and what he had learned from Henry Dietz, the groom Curry had fired for stealing watches. Charlie had talked to Jack Warner the previous day about hiring Dietz, and when Charlie saw the trainer that morning, Warner told him that Dietz would probably start work before the end of the week, although Warner swore he meant to keep a close eye on him to make sure he kept his nose clean. In any case, Krause and the four guards agreed that the starting point of their investigation ought to be Wayne Curry.

Rico agreed to find out where Wayne Curry had come from in Connecticut, then drive down and see if he could dig up any dirt. Tyler said he would see if there was anything to be learned from Curry's years on Dwyer's farm from friends he had on neighboring horse farms in Kentucky. Krause, Wanamaker, and Gillespie agreed to look around Saratoga, talk to people who worked for Curry, trying to find out what sort of person he was.

Having set this part of his investigation in motion, Charlie had then left the stable to seek out various gamblers he used to know in Saratoga in order to verify Chief Peterson's story about a move to reestablish gambling. After several hours, he had run across Max Tubbs, a thin dapper gambler of sixty-five from whom Charlie had once confiscated a dozen slot machines.

Tubbs would sometimes say the Max stood for Maxwell and sometimes for Maximilian, but generally he was known as Maximum Tubbs. He had begun gambling in Saratoga in 1931 and for the next twenty-one years, before Governor Dewey closed down the tables, he had accumulated enough money to make him rich—would have made him rich if he hadn't lost it just as quickly in other people's games. However, the habit of those years was such that Maximum Tubbs had tried to maintain his role as gambler ever since, which had led to frequent arrests and a friendship with Charlie Bradshaw.

Around three in the afternoon, Charlie found him dealing blackjack in the back of a Texaco station at the edge of town. Tubbs agreed, after some prodding, to find out about Ackerman and the current status of Saratoga gambling, then meet Charlie that evening at the Backstretch.

Charlie finished his thirtieth length and glanced at the clock. It was just 7:30. It took Charlie about twenty-two minutes to swim half a mile: thirty-six lengths. He was satisfied with that, although he knew it was about fifteen minutes longer than the record. Seeing the clock made him realize it was at this time that Ackerman often went swimming. Charlie would look up and there would be Lew spitting into his goggles at the edge of the pool or tightening the string of his green Speedo suit. If he saw Charlie looking, he would wave. If there was a lane free next to Charlie, Lew would take that one.

As he headed back up the pool, Charlie remembered the number "730," which Ackerman had written on his new blotter, and it again struck him as peculiar that Ackerman should have to remind himself when he swam. Then Charlie wondered why he had thought it signified a time. Probably because he had noticed it at about the same moment he came across the goggles in the top drawer of the desk. Actually, the number could be anything. It could even be a date. As this occurred to him, Charlie could feel his mind grow more alert. July 30th would be Sunday, two days away. Again, Charlie had the sense he was forgetting something, and with that was the fear that something as terrible as the murders was swimming toward him out of the future.

Charlie finished his half mile and climbed out of the pool.

138

As he showered and washed his hair, he kept thinking of the number on the blotter and the possibility that it was a date that had some connection with Ackerman's death. He dressed quickly, wanting to get to the Backstretch as soon as possible; but as he was leaving he happened to glance into the weight room, which was empty except for one man on the Universal. Only when he had gone a few steps past the door did Charlie realize that the man was Wayne Curry.

Charlie stopped, then went back to the doorway for a second look. Dressed in gym shoes and purple shorts, Curry was on his back on a bench repeatedly pulling the bar down to his midriff. Charlie knew little about the Universal, but guessed that the weights attached to the pulley weighed certainly more than fifty pounds. As if there were no weights at all, Curry lowered and raised his arms as easily as if he had been swimming. His muscular body was tanned and glistened with sweat. The pulley made a creak, then a rattling crash, over and over, as the weights returned to position.

Charlie continued to watch until he happened to glance further into the room and saw a mirror attached to the far wall. In the center of the mirror was Curry's lean face and Charlie realized the man was staring at him. Charlie started to look away, then didn't. Despite the effort and physical exertion of repeatedly pulling down the bar, Curry's face bore the same manikinlike nonexpression that had struck Charlie the previous day. It was only with difficulty that Charlie could make himself believe Curry was staring at him. Then, when he did, he grew embarrassed and hurried out of the building to find his car.

Five minutes later, Charlie was in his yellow Volkswagen on his way to the Backstretch. As he drove, he kept thinking of Curry staring at him in the weight room mirror, while in his memory the size of the weights increased until

139

it seemed that Curry had been effortlessly pulling two hundred pounds. It gave Charlie the immediate sense that he had no time to spare. Regretfully, he glanced down at the biography of Dillinger on the seat beside him. Just the sight of the half-finished book seemed to soothe him. He liked the fact that the anarchy and uncertainty of Dillinger's life could be arranged in 450 digestible pages.

It had pleased Charlie to discover that Dillinger had been a great second baseman, both for his home team in Martinsville, Indiana, and for the Indiana State Reformatory team in Pendleton. The governor had thought Dillinger good enough to play major league ball and transferred Dillinger to the state prison in Michigan City because it had the best prison team in Indiana.

Dillinger had been a strong White Sox fan and might have played for the White Sox had his life been different. He certainly could have been no worse, Charlie thought, than Shoeless Joe Jackson, Swede Risberg, Buck Weaver, Happy Felsch, and the other four White Sox players who had been paid $70,000 to throw the first two games of the 1919 World Series. Dillinger had been sixteen at the time and his criminal activity up until then had consisted of stealing coal from the Pennsylvania Railroad yards and selling it to neighbors.

Charlie pulled into the parking lot next to the Backstretch and cut the engine. Actually, he thought, it was a famous Saratoga gambler who had been accused, but never convicted, of masterminding the World Series fix. Arnold Rothstein, known in the city as Mr Big, had once owned the Brook, the most exclusive of the Saratoga casinos after World War I, as well as owning a stable of horses, and being the silent partner in a number of other casinos including the Chicago Club. Rothstein drank milk instead of whiskey, collected Whistler etchings, and employed Legs Diamond as his private killer. He was finally murdered in 1928 in the Park Central Hotel in New York City for refusing to pay the $320,000 he had lost in cards to Nigger Nate Raymond.

Rothstein sometimes reminded Charlie of Lew Ackerman, since both men began their fortunes by running poker games in New York as teenagers. But while Lew enjoyed people and had some sense of ethics, Rothstein had become involved in everything from industrial rackets to selling narcotics. Hours before he was shot, he had been in Lindy's where he wagered $500,000 that Herbert Hoover would defeat Al Smith in the imminent presidential election. Rothstein's lawyer once described him as like "a mouse standing in a doorway, waiting for his cheese." Nobody could ever have said that about Lew Ackerman.

Doris Bailes was behind the bar and smiled at Charlie as he came in. Seeing her and feeling the responding tension in his chest, Charlie once more regretted having a temperament formed by the romantic movies of the 1940s. He nodded and made his way to the pay phone near the entrance to the back room where the blond stripper was just taking her place on the stage. Charlie got Frank Warner's home phone number from information and dialed. He was hoping the trainer could shed light on the number 730, explain it away as a horse medicine or the best speed on six and a half furlongs. Frank answered as the juke box began blaring out "Boogie-oogie-oogie."

"Frank, this is Charlie, can you think of any reason that Lew would have written the number 730 on his blotter?"

There was a silence, then a suspicious voice which Charlie had to strain to hear: "Why? What's so important about it?"

"I'm not sure," said Charlie. "Lew wrote it down shortly before he was shot. It could be some perfectly innocent thing connected with the stable so I thought I'd ask you."

"I thought the police were handling the investigation."

"They are, but I just ran across this and thought it might be important."

"Doesn't ring any bells with me, Charlie. Where you calling from anyway?"

"A pay phone. What about as a date, you know, this Sunday? Do you know if he had anything planned for then?"

One of the two sailors from the naval base who were watching the stripper began to shout, "Take it all off, baby, take off the fuckin G-string. Let's see a little nookie." Charlie imagined Warner listening carefully so he could report it later to Charlie's cousins. It had only been about a month before that his middle cousin, Robert, had laid his hand on Charlie's shoulder and said, "Charlie, it makes me proud to say that in all my twenty-five years of marriage Lucy has never seen the inside of a saloon."

"No, Charlie," said Warner, "the number doesn't mean anything special. You know as well as I do that Sunday's the day before the track opens. Is that all you wanted? I've still got some work to do."

"Sure, Frank. Thanks."

Charlie made his way back to the bar and ordered a beer from Doris. She had on a white Mexican blouse and a Mexican tin necklace. The top three buttons of her blouse were undone, and her tan skin, the line of her breasts, made Charlie want to reach out and touch her. As he thought this, he wondered if he wasn't the corrupt and disreputable black sheep Warner thought him to be. For his first dozen years as a policeman, Charlie was constantly arresting aged drunks and derelicts who fondly claimed friendship with his father, remembering him as a man who would wager on anything.

142

Recalling this, Charlie also remembered his mother telling him that his father had bet a thousand dollars that Al Smith would defeat Herbert Hoover.

Charlie glanced at his watch. It was just past eight. Maximum Tubbs should be arriving shortly, while Victor had said he would stop by around 9:30. Charlie was worried about Victor. There appeared to be something bothering him apart from the attack of the night before. Charlie had asked him what was wrong, but Victor just brushed it off. He hoped Victor hadn't decided to return to New York or go live with his son in Chicago. Even though Frank Warner felt there was nobody more low class than Victor Plotz, Charlie knew he had no better friend in Saratoga.

Doris came over and wiped off the bar in front of him. "I like it when you've been swimming," she said, "it makes your ears all pink and shiny."

"Is that a good enough reason for you to come home with me tonight?"

"For gin rummy or sex?" Doris looked at Charlie steadily for a moment, then pushed her dark brown hair away from her eyes.

"Sex," said Charlie.

"You lost me there. I might have come for gin rummy."

"All right, gin rummy."

"Ah, Charlie, you've lost me again. You've got to stick to your guns."

Charlie looked down at his beer glass, then looked up again. "What about gin rummy and sex combined? Not only that, but I'll throw in an order of scrambled eggs and bacon."

"I've got enough trouble with my figure without eating all night, but if I had known you were so handy with a skillet I would have stopped by this morning. I jogged by your cottage around 6:30. Would I have been welcome?"

143

"Without a doubt," said Charlie. "A truly healthy person only requires four hours sleep a night."

"I'll remember that next time," said Doris.

Maximum Tubbs appeared about ten minutes later. He was a small, trim man with a full head of thick, steel gray hair and an immaculate blue seersucker suit. Before he sat down at a booth, he wiped off the seat and back with several napkins.

"Never know who's been sitting someplace," said Tubbs. "Germs are the enemies of old age."

Charlie ordered another beer and Tubbs had a Vichy with a twist of lime. He had clean, pink hands with long fingers that were never still but tapped and snapped and drummed on the table.

"So what did you find out?" asked Charlie once they were settled.

"I don't know where you got your information, Charlie, but that move to legalize gambling doesn't seem much greater than it ever is."

"I heard the state was looking into it."

"Well, they've got some committee, but there's no sign of its even meeting yet. It's true that Ackerman was dead set against gambling. He wanted Saratoga for the symphony and ballet. No more casinos." Tubbs paused to make sure his tie was straight. It was a dark blue tie with dozens of miniature white dice. "Maybe Ackerman would have appeared before this committee, but that would of been some time off."

"So you don't think Lew could have been murdered because of his opposition to gambling?"

"Who's to say," said Tubbs. "Gamblers are funny people. Ackerman was one himself. He ran a pretty big poker game before he quit."

"What about gambling interests on Long Island?"

144

"That's just the thing, Charlie. There're always gambling interests on Long Island that want to open up casinos in Saratoga and, sure, those people probably aren't too sorry that Ackerman is dead, but that's not to say they killed him. Personally, I think gambling's going to come back. I mean, it's bound to. But it's not going to happen tomorrow."

"What if gambling were legalized, where do you think the casinos would be?"

"That's hard to say," said Tubbs, looking critically at his thumbnail. "Maybe in some of the old mansions, like where the Chicago Club used to be. Maybe in the hotels. The Gideon Putnam could easily put in a casino. And there's a new hotel being planned that will make the Gideon Putnam look like small potatoes. It'd be built so a casino could be put right in and it'll have a big bar and restaurant and a stage show. You know, live acts straight from Las Vegas. They've already begun putting together the financing."

"Where's it going to be?"

"Don't know for sure. They're looking into a couple of sites. They want to have it near the Performing Arts Center. About as near to it as the Gideon Putnam. The whole thing's still pretty secret."

"Is Robert Dwyer involved in this by any chance?"

"That old guy? No, he's not. Funny you should ask though, because his son-in-law's into it pretty heavy. I forget his name."

"Wayne Curry."

"That's right. Curry. He's one of the big investors."

"Wouldn't these guys have to put up a lot of money?" asked Charlie.

"Damn right. A fortune."

18

"WHAT I BEEN THINKIN," said Victor, "is I wouldn't have to go to Chicago or back to New York. I might go down to Nashville instead. Make my fortune in the country music business."

"So what do you know about country music?" asked Charlie. They were in Charlie's Volkswagen driving along the eastern shore of Saratoga Lake. What he had learned about Curry and the proposed hotel had made Charlie decide to talk to Field one more time. It was past ten o'clock and to Charlie's right he could see a nearly full moon rising over the lake as he drove by darkened cottages and stores.

"Good grief, Charlie, music's my middle name. What do you think of this little number:

> *I'm not a man for candy,*
> *Don't tempt me with apple pie,*
> *You won't find me drinkin soda pop,*
> *Whiskey is all I try.*
> *I've lost my taste for sweet things*
> *Since you said goodbye."*

Victor sang in a high, clear falsetto that Charlie would not have guessed possible. The Volkswagen seemed to quiver on the road.

146

"So you're set on leaving Saratoga?" asked Charlie, keeping his tone of voice conversational.

"No, not set, I wouldn't say set. I just been thinkin about it, that's all. I'll make up my mind once we wrap up this investigation. You think Field will back you up now?"

"Perhaps. If I explain what we've found out about Curry, then maybe. But there's still a lot that doesn't make sense. I can't believe Curry had Ackerman killed or killed him himself just because of his objection to gambling in Saratoga. Also, where's Curry getting the money for the hotel?"

"I read of a guy once who killed his poor old grandmother because he didn't like how she ate her soup. What're you goin to do after you see Field?"

"I guess I'll try to find out where Lew went that Tuesday night."

Victor didn't respond to this but seemed to be staring out at the lake.

"You told me the other day you thought that was probably important," said Charlie. "Have you changed your mind?"

Victor remained silent. As they drove, the moon path kept up with them across the water, lighting up boats and the choppy waves stirred by a southern wind.

"Well," said Victor at last, "I may have made some trouble for you there."

"What do you mean?"

Victor rapped his knuckles on his cast, which was supported by a sling around his neck. "I mean maybe I know why I got my arm busted and when I tell you, maybe you'll want to bust the other one."

"What are you talking about?"

"I'm trying to say I think I found out where Ackerman went. You see, he turned up at the Backstretch on foot later on that Tuesday night. Then he got one of the regulars to

147

drive him home." Victor continued to explain how he had talked to the man who had given Ackerman a ride, how he had learned about Hyde Street and knocked on doors, how he had talked to Robert Dwyer and how it was only later when he learned more about Dwyer that he realized it might be important.

"I didn't want to say anything about it," said Victor, "until I checked those last six houses, but I checked them this afternoon and they'd seen Ackerman about as much as they'd seen Santa Claus or Rudolph Valentino. What I think is that he really went to Dwyer's, although maybe he didn't see Dwyer himself. Maybe he saw that Curry fellow. He's got the carriage house behind Dwyer's. I been lookin for him, but he wasn't there yesterday and he wasn't there today. Just some horsey guys sittin around and they didn't know nothin."

"You mean you just knocked on all the doors on Hyde Street and asked if Ackerman had been there for some reason that later got him killed?"

"Not exactly like that. I was pretty subtle."

"You're lucky you weren't killed last night," said Charlie. He couldn't believe Victor had ever been subtle in his life. "Then you went back today? You're not even safe to be around."

"Well, that's what I figured when I came to in the ambulance. I mean, I guess I lit a real fire under somebody."

"Jesus, Victor, you're the one who got burned."

"Vic," said Victor.

But Charlie was no longer paying attention. He was thinking about what Neal Claremon's wife had said about her husband's remark that there was nothing worse than a stable fire. Then, almost without transition, it occurred to Charlie that if Dwyer's stable burned and the insurance were paid off, then Curry would have both money and location for the new hotel. And again, almost without transition, there came to him the possible significance of the number 730 on Ackerman's blotter. The 30th was Sunday, only a day before the races, and the stable would be at its fullest and most valuable. Then Charlie asked himself, what if Claremon had found out there was going to be a fire and went to Ackerman with the information?

"You know," said Charlie, "I think I've just figured out what Curry's been doing."

But now it was Victor who wasn't paying attention. "What the hell's wrong with that asshole behind us that he won't dim his lights?"

For a few seconds, Charlie had been vaguely aware that the interior of the Volkswagen had grown quite bright. Glancing into the rearview mirror, he saw the four lights of what he guessed was a pickup truck about ten feet behind his rear bumper. Charlie slowed down and moved a little to the right. Instead of passing, however, the truck moved steadily closer until there was a metallic clang and jolt as it touched the back bumper.

"If that's another one of your asshole criminal friends," said Victor, "you can tell him from me to stop fuckin around. I like my jokes purely verbal."

Charlie didn't say anything but sped up slightly. The truck dropped back a few feet. It made a high roaring noise and Charlie guessed it was a four-speed in third gear. He turned his attention back to the highway, which was empty and dark. The pickup sped up again, hitting the bumper with a louder clang and making the Volkswagen swerve on the road.

"I expect," said Charlie, "that they're the same people who broke your arm."

Charlie accelerated to sixty, but the truck stayed inches behind him. The road along the lake curved one way, then another as it followed the shore. There wasn't enough space between the two vehicles to let Charlie either slow or turn without being rammed from behind. Charlie found himself thinking of a time ten years before when Chief Peterson sent him to Syracuse to attend a State Police training session on avoidance tactics in a high speed chase. Although Charlie knew how to execute a split-second U-turn at 120-miles-per-hour, he could think of nothing to do about an oversize pickup truck less than a foot away from a Volkswagen bumper. The four bright lights in his mirror were blinding. He reached out and tilted the mirror upward so he could see ahead more clearly. They had passed no other cars.

"Take a shot at them," said Victor. "Shoot right back through the back window and I'll pay for the damage."

"I'm not armed."

"You kiddin? I thought you always had a gun."

"I hardly ever carry one."

"Christ, Charlie, you cop types, I thought you'd feel naked unless you went out armed to the teeth. You mean we're stuck with this madman and all I can do is throw the roadmap at him?"

"That's about it."

The truck dropped back a few feet, then surged forward, smashing the rear of the Volkswagen so hard that it swerved onto the dirt shoulder, then back across the lane into the left lane as Charlie struggled to keep the car under control. Just as he managed to straighten the wheel, the truck again rushed forward, smashing into his bumper, and again he swerved to the right, then left. He heard the sound of breaking glass and bits of metal falling into the road, and irrelevantly he found himself thinking about the financial damage to the back of his car. At the same time, he couldn't

150

quite think what the truck wanted. Then he realized that was foolish. They weren't being threatened or frightened. This was going to be murder and as the truck roared ahead and smashed his bumper for yet another time, Charlie knew there was absolutely nothing he could do about it. Glancing at Victor, Charlie saw he had his hand flat against the dash and was pushing himself back in his seat. Beyond him through the window, Charlie caught sight of a small darkened grocery where he often stopped to buy Freihofer chocolate chip cookies if he felt thinner than usual and in need of soothing. The grocery now seemed to be a place in another country.

Then Charlie saw the trees and cottages drop away as the road rose slightly above the lake. At that moment he realized what the truck had been waiting for. There was now nothing between them and the water. As if his thought were a signal, the truck dropped back about five feet, then swerved out into the left lane and surged forward again with a roar. Charlie slammed on his brakes and tried to pull over, but it was no use. The truck swung sharply to the right, smashing the rear left fender of the Volkswagen and sending it rushing off the road as easily as a Ping-Pong ball.

Charlie was aware of a rising moan coming from Victor as the Volkswagen plunged and rattled down the bank toward the lake. Charlie knew the spot where they had gone off the road. Some distance ahead in the darkness was a small cliff maybe ten or fifteen feet above the lake where all summer he had seen teenagers diving into the water. The Volkswagen was sluing to the left and right as it rushed toward the drop. Charlie wrestled to straighten the wheel so at least they would go over the edge nose first. Although he had downshifted and kept pumping the brake, he guessed he was still going about forty. High grass whipped the sides

151

of the car. Charlie tried to think if he was terrified, but he was too busy to feel much of anything. He hated the way everything was bouncing around.

"Get ready to jump!" he shouted to Victor.

"I hate sports," said Victor, still pushing back with his hand on the dash.

Letting go of the wheel with his right hand, Charlie quickly swung out and hit Victor across the face. "Victor, you've got to jump!"

The car plunged over the small cliff and for a moment everything was silent, while ahead of them the lights showed nothing but miles of black water.

"Jump!" shouted Charlie.

He opened the door of the Volkswagen, pulled himself out with his fingers gripping the roof and pushed himself upward. Briefly, his feet caught against the pedals, then against the steering wheel, but by this time his body was above the surface of the car and so when the car hit the water, Charlie was thrown forward and free. He curled his body, tucking his knees under his chin, and for a few seconds skimmed along the surface like a skipped stone. Then he went under.

Unable to help himself, Charlie began to choke and breathe in water as his water-soaked clothes dragged him deeper and deeper beneath the surface. The blackness was like death and for the first time that evening he felt panic and began to kick and thrash his arms. Then he took hold of himself and tried to relax. He told himself that water wasn't strange to him, that he swam several miles each week. He kicked off his shoes, slipped out of his jacket and pants and at last floated up to the surface. Then he began swimming back to the Volkswagen and Victor. His great fear was that Victor was dead or trapped inside unable to get out. He pushed away the thought and swam rapidly

152

through the water to where in the moonlight he saw masses of white bubbles and steam rising from his car. Looking further, he saw flashlights bobbing along the shore.

Charlie guessed the Volkswagen was down about ten feet. Taking a deep breath, he dove into the bubbles. He could see nothing but after a moment he touched the roof of the car. Almost immediately something grabbed him, seemingly tried to drag him deeper. Although he knew it was Victor, the attack was so fierce and violent that Charlie again had to force himself not to panic. Victor was clutching one of his legs, trying to claw his way up Charlie's body. Charlie twisted himself so his feet were on the roof of the car, while with his right hand he reached down and caught hold of Victor's collar, both keeping him from climbing any higher or getting away. It was fortunate, Charlie knew, that Victor only had the use of one arm. With two, he wouldn't be able to control him.

Charlie pushed his feet against the roof of the car, trying to drag Victor up with him, but Victor wouldn't budge. Again he tried to push himself upward, but Victor still wouldn't come free. Charlie guessed he was caught in the door. There was no time to dive down and free him even if he could loosen Victor's grip. Charlie's lungs ached and he was desperate for air. Bending his knees, he let Victor pull him down to the roof of the car as Victor frantically clawed his way upward and at last circled Charlie's head with his arm. Then Charlie pushed with all his strength against the Volkswagen roof. At first nothing happened, but then Victor came free. Charlie began to kick desperately, using his one arm to pull himself through the water. When he broke the surface, he took great gasping breaths. He slipped his head free of Victor's wrestling hold, pushed him away and rolled over on his back.

There was a shout and, glancing toward Victor, Charlie

saw him thrashing and slowly sinking beneath the surface. Charlie rolled over, kicked his way toward him, and grabbed Victor's good arm just as it disappeared.

Resurfacing, Victor began clawing his way up Charlie's arm. Charlie drew up his legs and kicked Victor away; then, grabbing his collar, he held him at arm's length as he pedaled his feet to keep his head above water.

"Can't you swim?" shouted Charlie.

Victor shook his head and tried to shout something.

"Try to relax and I'll tow you in. Don't fight me or I'll leave you."

It was only about twenty-five feet to shore. Charlie turned Victor over on his back and, again grabbing his collar, slowly towed him in to where he could see a group of people with flashlights. Victor kept coughing and spitting up water. Charlie thought how beautiful the lake looked with the moonlight shimmering on its surface. Then he thought of his yellow Volkswagen. He had prided himself on the fact it had no dents, scratches, or rust. After that it occurred to him that someone had tried to kill him.

When the water was waist deep, he let go of Victor and stood up. Victor stood beside him. Charlie could hear his teeth chattering.

"You saved my life," said Victor, shivering. "I thought that only happened on the TV."

"I didn't want to take care of your cat."

"Hey, Charlie, you watch out or you'll find yourself with a sense of humor."

"Heaven forbid," said Charlie.

What angered Charlie more than having his car run off the road was the fact the police lieutenant required him to take a blood test.

154

"I'm not drunk and I haven't been drinking. I already told you what happened. We were bumped off the road by a pickup truck. Somebody tried to kill us."

"Look, Bradshaw, it's part of the routine. If you refuse to take the test, I can only assume you have something to hide."

They had been brought into the police station and stood dripping in front of the desk. Both Victor and Charlie had gray army blankets draped over their shoulders. On the bench behind them, an old woman whose drinking had caused her to be kicked out of bars for the past fifty years kept saying: "Don't take it so hard. Troubles happen to the best of us."

The lieutenant was a sandy-haired, sandy-faced, ex-military policeman named Schultz. Peterson had hired him and advanced him because of his military background. Charlie had never liked him nor liked the way he bullied prisoners.

"Sure I'll take the test, but you better put out an alert for that truck. It'll have yellow paint marks on the right front fender."

"Yeah, yeah, I've called the state boys."

When Peterson arrived at midnight, Charlie and Victor were preparing to leave police headquarters dressed in some old clothes. Peterson made them wait while he talked to Schultz who had become more obliging after receiving proof that Charlie was sober.

"Now, Charlie," said Peterson as he came out to where Charlie and Victor were waiting, "what's all this about your being bumped off the road?"

Charlie could tell by his tone that Peterson was ready to make up and be, if not friendly, as least cordial. Even at this hour, he was dressed in his impeccable blue suit. Charlie on the other hand had little interest in making up. All he cared about was getting home and getting to bed.

"I already told Schultz. It looked like a large three-quarter-ton truck. I couldn't determine the color, but if you drag my car out of the lake you can get paint samples from where the truck hit me."

"Why would anyone want to knock you into the lake?"

"That's what I intend to find out," said Charlie.

"Now, Charlie, you know it's your duty to tell us what you've found out. Does this have anything to do with Ackerman?"

Until this moment, Charlie hadn't realized how he felt betrayed by a police department to which he had given twenty years of his life. Having to take the blood test, instead of Schultz accepting his word, simply galled him.

"Peterson," he said, "I wouldn't tell you a thing."

"Damn right," said Victor, "that's what I like to hear."

19

"THAT'S RIGHT, it was a clear case of hit-and-run. Knocked the kid off his bike. Lucky it didn't kill him."

"Did he do time for it?" asked Charlie.

"No, his old man's got some money," said Rico. "Must of paid a bundle to keep Curry out of jail."

"And when was all this?"

"Fall of '71," said Rico. "He'd been out of the army about a month."

Rico was calling from Greenwich, Connecticut. It was about four o'clock Saturday afternoon and Charlie was in his office at Lorelei Stables. Outside some of the exercise boys were throwing a Frisbee and Charlie could hear them calling to each other in Spanish.

Rico had learned that Curry had gone to a private boys' school, quit in his junior year to hitchhike out to California, joined the army, and got into the Green Berets, served three tours in Viet Nam, and came out a lieutenant in 1971. The hit-and-run accusation appeared to be the one thing against him and it had never been proved in court.

"It must of been his father that got him the job at Belmont, some kind of public relations thing. He'd only had it a couple of months when he met Dwyer's daughter."

"And they were married fairly quickly?"

"That's right. Two weeks after they met. Curry quit his job."

"What's his relationship with his family now?" asked Charlie.

"Seems pretty nonexistent. Least he's never down here. His mother died in '70 and the father remarried about four years later. You want me to dig around and find out?"

"No, come on back up. We'll need you tonight."

After Charlie hung up, he walked to the door of his office. In the ten yards between his corner of the barn and the training track, about a dozen different colored Frisbees were spinning through the air, while his youngest guard, Eddie Gillespie, was in the act of vaulting the fence to the track to retrieve a red Frisbee that lay in the dirt.

Earlier Gillespie and John Wanamaker had stopped by to tell Charlie what they had learned about Wayne Curry in Saratoga. There hadn't been much. Curry was active in the country club and a number of civic organizations. His friends tended to be wealthy: men who had made their money in real estate speculation, construction, investments. Four times a year, when his wife visited from California, Curry would throw large catered dinner parties. He appeared to have no close friends or cronies.

After telling Gillespie and Wanamaker he would need them that evening, he let them go. It seemed interesting to Charlie that Curry appeared to know no gamblers or race track people, and moved in entirely different social circles than his father-in-law.

For the first time that week, Charlie felt comfortable about the relationship of his actions to the world around him. His earlier sense that something was being overlooked had disappeared when Victor confessed to his own investigation, while getting run off the road was at least proof that

158

his assumptions about Ackerman's death were generally accurate. The previous night Charlie had decided it would be dangerous to go home, so he and Victor had slept on cots at the stable. While there, they had worked out a plan of action for the coming evening which, if it worked, would put Curry behind bars for good.

But even as he stood in the doorway congratulating himself on his grasp of events, Charlie knew there were two points of confusion which indicated there was information still unaccounted for. The first was something which had happened to Dwyer and the second was the fact that Curry was going to great lengths to make people think Charlie was crazy. He had discovered this when he saw Field that morning.

Charlie had borrowed Victor's Dodge Dart and had driven out to Field's to explain his interpretation of the case and to convince Field to give him backing. This time Field received him in his living room which had a wall of glass facing the lake. The view, to Charlie, was nearly overpowering. He could even see the spot where he had been knocked into the water. Earlier Charlie had directed a tow truck and diver to the site, and as Charlie talked to Field he kept glancing northward to where his yellow Volkswagen was being removed from the lake.

"You could have been killed," said Field.

"That was the point."

"I still don't see why you can't turn your information over to the police." Field was sitting in a deep armchair in the darkest corner of the room. The albino Doberman lay at his feet staring at Charlie. Whenever Charlie spoke, the dog would growl very quietly. The noise was like a purr.

"Peterson is pursuing his own investigation and hasn't shown himself interested in what I have to say. Also he's a close friend of Dwyer's and thinks my interest in Dwyer, or rather Curry, is an attempt to make him look bad. If I am right that Curry intends to burn the stable either tonight or tomorrow night, then I would rather catch him myself than let Peterson bungle it."

"Don't you think you're being controlled too much by your feelings?" asked Field. "Why not tell Peterson about the fire?"

"Because I have no evidence it will take place. A comment that a groom makes to his wife, a number on a blotter, Curry's plan to build a hotel and the possible future of gambling in Saratoga—Peterson would just laugh at it."

Field's narrow gray face appeared concerned and uncertain. Looking at the sad gray eyes, Charlie grew irritated with himself for ever thinking the accountant a cold man.

"You know that Curry called this morning to complain about you?" asked Field.

At first Charlie didn't think he had heard correctly. "Called to complain about me?"

"That's right."

"What did he say?"

"That you'd been badgering both him and Dwyer with your suspicions about Ackerman's death. He said he didn't care himself, but it was upsetting to his father-in-law, who isn't well. He asked me if I thought you were all right in the head, that you had gone both to the stable and his house, that he had talked to the police about it and was preparing to get a court injunction. He also said he knew I was willing to sell Lorelei Stables and he was willing to make an offer, but because of your accusations he didn't want to do anything until the real murderer was caught. Why do you think he told me all that?"

Charlie wasn't sure. He couldn't imagine why Curry had

decided to draw attention to himself. It was at this point Charlie began to wonder if he was leaving something out. Through the window to his right, he saw a flash of yellow as the top of his Volkswagen broke the surface of the water. That at least was not something he had made up.

"I guess he's trying to make me look bad, maybe get you to fire me. Did you believe him?"

"He made it sound quite believable. On the other hand, Lew had a lot of faith in you. Let's say I believe Lew, even though I've known him to be mistaken. You think Curry shot Lew himself?"

"I think Lew went to him on that Tuesday night and told him he had heard he intended to burn Dwyer's stable. He probably thought that would be enough to keep Curry from doing it. What Lew may not have known was that Curry had already committed himself to paying large sums of money that he could only get if he had a fire. Curry lifts weights at the Y. He could easily calculate the difficulty of killing someone in the pool."

"Charlie, go to the police."

"Give me until August first. If there's no fire, then I'll go to Peterson. Thanks to Victor, Curry thinks I'm a bungler. Well, maybe I am, but we've got more information about him than he has any idea of. Hopefully, he'll go ahead with his plans. If he does, well, I've got six people plus myself and we could get the police and fire department over there in three or four minutes."

As Charlie stopped speaking, he again heard the dog growl. Lying at Field's feet in the dimmest part of the room, it looked more like the ghost of a Doberman.

"And if it goes wrong and you're arrested, then I'm supposed to say you're working for me. Is that right?"

"I'm hoping nothing so extreme will happen."

"Charlie, at this point, I want to sell and get out. Do what you have to, but don't do anything to interfere with that. I don't like it around here without Ackerman."

A few minutes later, as he had driven out of Field's driveway, Charlie saw Emmett Van Brunt parked along the side of the road in an unmarked blue Chevrolet. The policeman ducked down when Charlie pulled out and Charlie pretended not to have seen him.

The road curved right after Field's driveway and the moment the Chevrolet was out of sight, Charlie parked the Dodge Dart and ran back along the shoulder. Van Brunt neither saw nor heard him coming. When Charlie reached the police car, Emmett was talking into the radio.

"Yeah, he just left. You want me to follow him? Jesus, Chief, I don't see why you don't throw his ass in jail. That's a shame about Mr. Dwyer. You think he'll pull through?" There was a pause, then Emmett said, "All right, I'll head over there."

Van Brunt returned the microphone and started the car. Charlie stood right behind him at the open window. "What's this about Dwyer?" he asked.

Van Brunt turned in his seat so quickly that he cracked his elbow against the steering wheel. He began rubbing it furiously. "Jesus, Charlie, people like you should be locked up." Van Brunt kept his head turned away, still concentrating on his elbow. He wore a sport coat of green, yellow, and brown plaid.

"What about Dwyer?" asked Charlie. "Come on, Emmett, tell me what happened?"

"You won't get anything from me, Charlie. I know your tricks." Van Brunt rolled up the window, then put the Chevrolet in gear and drove off, leaving Charlie standing at the side of the road.

Charlie shrugged and walked back to Victor's car. He

wondered what sort of tricks he was capable of and if he could make a living at them after someone bought Lorelei Stables and he lost his job.

For the rest of the morning, Charlie had looked for an ex-torch he used to know in order to determine the best way to burn a stable. The man had once burned empty buildings for a group of realtors in Albany. When finally arrested, he had received a light sentence in return for testifying against his former employers. He was a small fat man and after his release he devoted his life to hanging around the sleazier Saratoga bars discussing the intricacies of arson. Charlie went to a half a dozen of these bars trying to find him only to learn he had apparently moved out to the West Coast.

Charlie had also tried to learn what had happened to Dwyer. Without much difficulty, he found out Dwyer had been rushed to the hospital in the middle of the night, but despite a number of phone calls he couldn't discover why, whether it had been another stroke or if he had fallen downstairs. All he could learn was that Dwyer was still in intensive care.

Instead of locating the ex-torch, Charlie himself was found by his cousin Jack only moments after he had gone up onto Broadway to buy a paper. It seemed that whenever he set foot on Broadway he was grabbed by people he wanted to avoid.

Actually, Jack was the cousin Charlie liked best, even though he had made his childhood the greatest misery. Jack was a year older and the owner of a successful hardware store. What made him difficult to be around as a child was that he did everything right, was always good humored, never sick, received letters in three sports, and slept with the window open throughout the winter. He helped Charlie with his homework, gave him clothes he'd grown out of himself, and introduced him to the girls he didn't want.

He had been a boy without impure thoughts, and Charlie, for whom impure thoughts seemed a way of life, had felt bullied.

Later Jack married an intelligent and beautiful woman, had three sons who became Little League stars, and twice received civic awards for service to the community. Although Charlie would have been shocked to discover his cousin dealt narcotics or did dirty things to little boys, it would have made him easier to bear.

This morning Jack was concerned because he had spoken to Frank Warner and learned that Field wanted to sell Lorelei Stables.

"I wanted to tell you, Charlie, you've no reason to worry about your future. If you're interested, there'll always be a place for you at the hardware."

"Thanks, Jack, I appreciate that." Despite his words, it was with a sense of relief that Charlie realized the offer meant nothing to him. Not long before such an offer would have made him crawl along the sidewalk in gratitude.

"You know, we have a type of profit-sharing plan so the more willing you are to work, the more you earn."

"That's great, Jack, that really is."

They stood on the sidewalk between city hall and the newsstand. Jack was about five inches taller than Charlie with wavy brown hair and wore khakis and a tattersall shirt from L. L. Bean's. His chin was as square and ruddy as the end of a brick. As he talked to Charlie, he kept pausing to wave to people he knew.

"Another thing, Charlie, you know a man by the name of Wayne Curry? He's Bob Dwyer's son-in-law. Now there's a grand old man for you. Where would Saratoga be without him?"

"Where indeed?" asked Charlie. "What's this about Curry?"

"He was in the store yesterday buying some rope and he asked if I knew any reason you might be holding a grudge against him and his father-in-law. I gathered he thought you'd been bothering them in some way and that old man Dwyer was upset. Is that true, Charlie?"

"Well, you know, Jack, I've been helping Peterson with the Ackerman murder and of course I've had to ask Curry and Dwyer some questions." Charlie said this off the top of his head while wondering what Curry was up to. Even so it sometimes surprised him how easily he could lie.

"Dwyer's got a lot of friends in this town, Charlie. You don't want to get him mad."

"You don't have to worry about me, Jack."

"And how have you been generally, Charlie? Staying out of trouble?"

"You better believe it."

"And your mother? She's a great old lady."

"She's made a bundle on this racehorse. Now she wants to come back in October and open a fancy whorehouse. I might get a job as bouncer."

A shadow flitted across Jack's high forehead as if he were experiencing a pain, then he smiled. "You were always a joker, Charlie."

"That's me," said Charlie.

It wasn't until he had returned to his office in the early afternoon that Charlie learned what happened to Dwyer. Victor had been sitting behind the desk with his feet up on the blotter. Leaning against the wall beside him was a small-bore pump gun. Charlie recognized it as belonging to Ackerman. It had been one of Ackerman's vanities that he was an excellent shot. Consequently, he prided himself on never firing anything heavier than this .410 when he went

165

bird hunting in the fall. And even though he used nothing but 2½-inch shells, he always brought back more birds than his friends armed with .12 or .20 gauge shotguns.

"From now on," said Victor, "I'm not going anyplace without this old equalizer. Who'd give my cat the kind of lovin he deserves if I got killed?"

Charlie sat down on the wooden chair across from Victor. "Can you think of any reason why Dwyer should be in the hospital? He was taken there in the middle of the night and I can't find out why."

"Maybe he was run off the road by a pickup truck."

"I'm serious."

"Why d'you think it's important?"

"I won't know if it's important until I find out why he's there, but it seems too much to believe that it's a coincidence."

Victor tapped a pencil against his cast which was already covered with multicolored hearts and signatures. "Well, maybe I can find out. Hold on." He leafed through the telephone book until he found a number, then he dialed. After a moment, he said, "Hey, Mac, why's Dwyer in the hospital? Okay, call me back." He read out his number, then hung up.

"Who was that?" asked Charlie.

Victor put one finger to his sealed lips and shook his head. A few minutes later the telephone rang and Victor picked it up. After listening for a moment, he said, "Yeah? You don't say. Jesus, what's the world coming to? Sure, I'll tell him you said hello."

Victor hung up the phone. "Took an overdose of pills. They pumped him out, but he's still in a coma. It's not certain he'll recover."

"A suicide attempt?"

"That's what it looks like."

166

"How'd you find that out?" asked Charlie.

Victor looked at his fingernails. "I called that orderly, that old murderer of yours. What's the point of knowing hoods if you don't make use of them?"

Charlie stared at Victor for a moment. He felt outmaneuvered in a way he couldn't quite put his finger on. "What did Dwyer seem like the other day?" he asked.

Victor scratched his elbows. "I don't know. Not a lotta laugh lines."

"I bet your visit raised a lot of questions in his mind."

"That's the kind of guy I am," said Victor.

Charlie asked himself what Dwyer would have done if he came to believe that his son-in-law was responsible for Ackerman's death. He remembered how he had been the other day: fragile, slightly wandering, thinking about the old times when he and Ackerman had been friendly competitors. He thought of him delivering the eulogy at Ackerman's funeral with Curry standing behind his wheelchair like a soldier at attention. He imagined the old man coming to the realization that Curry had murdered his old friend and then trying to live with it. On the other hand, perhaps Dwyer had never taken an overdose, perhaps it had been administered to him.

"You know," said Victor, "I once knew a guy that tried to asphyxiate himself with a motorcycle in a garage."

"Did it work?"

"Nah, we found him the next morning readin his way through a stack of old *Collier's* with the motorcycle still chuggin away. He said he had a headache, but I figured it was from readin in that bad light."

"Are you ever serious?" asked Charlie.

"Only when I'm bein beat up or drowned."

After he talked to Rico on the phone that afternoon, Charlie drove to the Backstretch to meet Phil Tyler, the

167

one guard he had not yet heard from. It was a warm and sunny Saturday afternoon and as he drove down Union Avenue past the track, he saw that black metal kettles of red geraniums had been hung around the old white gingerbread grandstand. Sprinklers watered the garden in the center of the track and swans busied themselves on the small lake.

In forty hours the track would open and Charlie and about thirty thousand others would crowd into the grounds. Until the first race, anything was possible, all systems of symbolism and logic pointing to the most improbable winners were full of promise. At that very moment racing addicts all over the East were attuning themselves to receive important messages from the ether: the licenses of cars which nearly hit them, a marred date on a shiny penny—numbers which on Monday would be translated into winners.

Charlie carefully studied the past performances in the *Racing Form*, studied training records, inspected the horses from hock to muzzle, but when he made his decision he knew the part of him which did the choosing was the same part which years before in high school had led him into unfortunate crushes on fast fat girls.

As he passed the paddock and track grounds and drew up to the light at Nelson Avenue, Charlie heard a siren and looked in his mirror in time to see Peterson's black Buick swerve around him. Instead of passing him, however, it swerved across his path and squealed to a halt. Since Charlie was sitting at a stop light and in any case wouldn't have considered making a run for it, he couldn't see the point of Peterson's melodramatics.

Peterson jumped out of the police car and stalked back toward the Dodge Dart. He looked like a man eager to break something. As he bent over to look in Charlie's window, the silver chain across the blue vest of his three-

168

piece suit fell forward and from it dangled a miniature silver revolver.

"You hear about Dwyer?" he demanded.

"Just this afternoon. Is he going to pull through?"

"I doubt it. You know whose fault it is that he's in there?" He paused, but before Charlie could answer, Peterson surged ahead again: "It's yours, Bradshaw. Curry told me how you been hounding the old man, making him suspicious and miserable. You know he's not strong in the head. He was sick and depressed and you had to make it worse. People don't think much of you around here, Bradshaw, and after this you'll be nothing: a fat zero. All I'm hoping is that you give me reason to pull you in. I'd love to turn the key on you."

Before Charlie could reply, Peterson stormed back to his car and squealed away, leaving about ten thousand miles of rubber in the intersection. Charlie wished he had Victor's ability to tell the world to kiss his ass. He found himself thinking of an El Paso cowboy by the name of "Cowboy" Bob Rennick, a little man who was rarely armed and had the reputation for being a dude. On the night in question— April 14, 1885—he had just bought himself a large white cowboy hat, of which he was overly proud, and had gone to the Gem Saloon to show it off. There, unfortunately, he met Bill Raynor, a former lawman and constant troublemaker who was known as "the best dressed bad man in Texas." Raynor proceeded to make fun of Cowboy Bob's hat, pointing out its various comic possibilities and adding that if he didn't like what he was saying, then Cowboy Bob could fight. Raynor had been involved in many gunfights and always won. Too frightened to speak up, Cowboy Bob indicated he was unarmed and with a snort of disgust Raynor wandered into the billiard room.

Cowboy Bob then ordered a couple of drinks, bolted them

down, and announced in a loud voice, "I've been imposed upon enough and won't stand for it." Then he snatched a revolver from the faro dealer. Seeing that Cowboy Bob was now armed, Raynor rushed into the bar with his guns blazing—"guns blazing" was a combination of words that always made Charlie breathe a little faster. Cowboy Bob knelt down and fired two shots, hitting Raynor in the stomach and shoulder. Mortally wounded, Raynor urged the bystanders to tell his mother he "died game." As he watched Peterson's black Buick disappear up Union Avenue, Charlie said to himself: "I've been imposed upon enough and won't stand for it."

By the time Charlie reached the Backstretch, it was past six. Phil Tyler was drinking a Jenny and Charlie sat down on the stool beside him.

"How you doin, old buddy?" asked Tyler.

Although Charlie didn't choke up, it was nice to hear someone express affection for him, even though that someone in his unreformed state had bilked dozens of citizens out of their savings by convincing them to buy nonexistent acreage in paradise. Tyler was tall, thin, dressed like a cowboy in jeans and a jean shirt, had long gray hair that touched his shoulders and a gray gunfighter's moustache. He always spoke quietly and delicately.

"You find out anything about Curry in Kentucky?" asked Charlie.

"Little bit, not much. He ran Dwyer's farm for a couple of years and all I could find out was he didn't like it and wasn't very good at it."

"How come Dwyer kept him on?"

"I don't think he heard about it. Curry was good at finding people who knew the business. The guy I talked to said he'd met him at a couple of parties. People down there like horses and Curry didn't, that's all it amounts to."

170

Charlie ordered a beer from Berney McQuilkin, then turned back to Tyler who was cleaning his nails with a jackknife. "You ready for tonight?" asked Charlie.

"Sure thing. We meet in your office at ten. We going to be armed?"

"Me and Krause are the only ones with licenses. Maybe we'll take a rifle as well." Remembering Peterson's expressed desire to lock him up, Charlie felt uncomfortable about trespassing with six armed men.

"I used to be pretty hot stuff with a rifle," said Tyler. "I bet I could shoot the match right out of Curry's hand."

"I'll remember that," said Charlie.

After Tyler left, Charlie sat drinking another beer. Doris hadn't come in yet and he kept glancing at the front door every time it opened. That night, if nothing went wrong, he and his guards would try to catch Curry burning Dwyer's stable. Part of Charlie kept urging him to turn it over to the police, but even if the police had been friendly and welcoming it's unlikely that he would have gone to them. In these warm days before the opening of the track, Charlie had moved through Saratoga as if the ghost of Ackerman were accompanying him. They were soft days, the sort of days that made Charlie recall the time when Broadway was lined with wineglass elms, when he could walk from one end to the other and count over five hundred men in Panama hats seated in rockers on the piazzas of the old hotels. Whoever had killed Ackerman, Charlie wanted to catch him himself.

His plan was to have two men go into the stable area with radios, while the other five waited outside. If either of the two saw anything suspicious, they would call Charlie, who would contact the police and the fire department on the CB. The other guards would then try to keep Curry and his associates from getting away. It would be a full moon that night and if Curry tried to start a fire, he would certainly be seen. Charlie felt fairly confident about this plan. His only question concerned Curry's reasons for telling people that Charlie was harassing him and was, in part, the cause of Dwyer's suicide attempt. It seemed eventually this could only draw attention to Curry himself.

Charlie was startled by a touch on the shoulder and, turning, he saw Doris sitting down on the stool beside him.

"I've got a few minutes before I start," she said. "Mind if I join you?"

"Not at all. Tell me, would you like me better if I was the manager of a hardware store?"

"No, I wouldn't. Are you planning to become one?"

"Not necessarily. What about an insurance and real estate executive or the foreman of a construction company, would you like me better then?"

"Can't say that I would." Doris was half turned toward Charlie. She wore a red bandanna over her brown hair and had on a white blouse and a blue denim skirt. Her face, framed by the bandanna, looked cheerful and expectant.

"I was afraid of that," said Charlie. "Then tell me this, will you go to the races with me on Monday? Red Fox is running in the fifth."

"Is Red Fox that Jesse James's horse?"

"That's right. Red Fox is the only horse in the world. No horse looks stronger or handsomer. That doesn't mean he'll win, but right now he's a champion."

"Do you think he'll win?"

"Of course I do, but that doesn't mean much. That's the trouble with horse racing. Will you come?"

"I'd be glad to."

Charlie was so startled he hardly thought he had heard her correctly. "You mean it?"

"Would you believe me any more if I put it in writing?"

172

"No, your word's good enough. I can't tell you how pleased I am that we'll see Red Fox lose together."

As he said this, Charlie was aware of someone else sitting down on the other side of him. Turning, he saw it was Jack Krause.

"What's up?" asked Charlie.

"I been talking to Vic," said Krause, "and I've decided to stick by you until all this gets finished. Sorry for the inconvenience, but I don't want you to get shot as well." Krause flicked a cigarette butt off the bar as if to signify Charlie's getting shot.

Charlie felt both touched and irritated. Turning back to Doris, he noticed she was halfway around the bar. When she saw him looking, she said, "Don't forget, I'm holding you to Monday."

Not only would Krause be upset if he were shot, thought Charlie, but it would be truly bad luck to be killed just when Doris had agreed to go out with him.

20

"SURE," SAID CHARLIE, "Owney Madden, Dutch
Schultz, Johnny Torrio, Lucky Luciano—they had the syndicate that controlled the casinos. Luciano ran the Chicago
Club himself. Took in $250,000 every August. They usually
kept Schultz off the floor. In the early thirties, the Chicago
Club was the classiest and most expensive club in town and
Dutch Schultz held it as a matter of religious faith that it
was a crime to pay more than two dollars for a shirt. Then
Schultz decided he had to rub out Thomas Dewey who was
busting up his rackets in New York, and Luciano knew
that would bring a lot of heat down on the syndicate, so he
told Anastasia at Murder, Inc., to get rid of Schultz. Actually, it was Charlie 'The Bug' Workman who shot Schultz
in the john of the Palace Chophouse in Newark while
Schultz was taking a leak."

Krause rubbed his big left fist along the line of his jaw.
"How come you know this stuff?" he said.

"I don't know. I read about it, then I like to go over it
in my mind," said Charlie. "It's like knitting."

Charlie and Krause were driving out to Charlie's cottage
in Victor's Dodge Dart in order to get Charlie's revolver.
It was about 9:30 Saturday evening and Charlie wanted to

get over to Dwyer's by eleven. Nervously, he kept looking in the rearview mirror, but the road behind him was clear. It was a full moon and so bright that Charlie felt he could drive without lights.

"Nice night," said Charlie.

Krause grunted, then took an immaculate white handkerchief from the breast pocket of his suit coat, delicately blew his nose in three little puffs and refolded the handkerchief. "Victor tells me you think Curry killed Lew, is that right?" asked Krause.

"I'm not so sure," said Charlie.

"When do you think you're going to be sure?"

Charlie knew what was coming and tried to be evasive. "Maybe tonight or tomorrow night, but we won't really be sure until we see him sent up for it."

"Remember what I asked, that's all. If Curry's the guy, then you gotta let me kill him. No sweat, I'll just put a bullet in his head." Krause patted a spot at his waist where Charlie assumed he was carrying his revolver.

"I'm not working for you," said Charlie, "and I can't just let you murder a man."

"You working for Field?"

"I guess I'm working for myself," said Charlie as he slowed for his driveway.

"Bet you don't get paid much," said Krause.

Charlie parked and they got out of the car. As they walked across the gravel to the house, Krause said, "I once fought Joey Maxim right after the war. That was years before he became light heavyweight champion. It was my biggest fight and the farthest I ever got. Because I'd been around a while and'd won my last couple of fights, I was the favorite. Maxim, he got in the ring and he walked all over me. I was out by the fourth round."

Krause paused. His forehead protruded slightly and in the moonlight it shone almost white, while the lower part of his face was dark.

"A writer for some rag in New York said I'd thrown the fight," Krause continued. "Shit, I didn't throw no fight. Maxim was a better fighter, that's all. Well, this writer kept suggesting I'd taken a dive and one night I ran into him in a bar, like I was coming back from the juke box and he was passing in the other direction. He gave me a bad look and I grabbed his shirt. He just smiled. He knew if I hit him I'd be outta boxing forever. No training camp jobs, no nothing. Besides which, I'd land in jail. So I let him go. He called me something I didn't catch and left. After that, right up till I quit boxing, he always wrote bad about me. I've always regretted not punching him. Just one punch to the head. It would of been worth the jail and no boxing. Just one punch to the head. When someone hurts you, you gotta hurt them back. What I'm saying, Charlie, if Curry's the one, you gotta let me have him. Understand?"

They had been standing at Charlie's front door while Charlie hunted for the key and swatted mosquitoes. At last Charlie unlocked the door and they went inside. "I understand you well enough," he said, "I'm just not going to help you do it. Excuse the mess." Discarded shirts, pants, shoes, and about eight socks were scattered across the living room floor. "I haven't had time to clean up."

Going into the kitchen, Charlie opened the drawer by the sink where he kept his .38 in its holster. The revolver was empty and Charlie loaded it, taking a box of shells from on top of the kitchen cabinet. Then he attached the holster to his belt, put a few extra shells in his coat pocket, and returned to the living room where Krause was staring out at the moonlight on the lake.

"You think you'll use that gun tonight?" asked Krause.

176

"I hope not," said Charlie. "I'm a rotten shot." He picked up a blue shirt off the floor, laid it across the back of a chair, then shrugged. "Let's go," he said.

As they turned toward the door, however, a pair of headlights swung into Charlie's driveway, drew up behind the Dodge Dart and blinked out.

"You expecting anyone?" asked Krause.

Charlie didn't answer but listened to the sound of a single pair of feet walking across the gravel toward the house. At first Charlie thought it might be Peterson, then he thought it might be Rico who still had not returned from Connecticut. Charlie flicked on the porch light and opened the door. Wayne Curry stood on the steps.

Curry looked at him with his pale blue eyes in a way Charlie was getting used to. "I want to talk to you, Bradshaw."

Charlie stood aside and let Curry enter. Krause stood by the window and watched. He seemed very still. Charlie shut the door and followed Curry into the room. "What do you want to talk about?" he asked.

"I want to know what you have against me."

"What makes you think I've got anything against you?" asked Charlie.

"You've been bothering the people who work for me and you've been bothering Mr. Dwyer. He's a sick man, don't you know that? That friend of yours really upset him. If he dies, then a lot of people are going to think you're responsible. You think I killed Ackerman? Come on, tell it to my face."

Charlie leaned against the doorway to the kitchen. He was uncertain why Curry had come and as he thought about it, he became increasingly uncomfortable. "Why did Lew Ackerman visit you three nights before he was killed?"

"Is that what's worrying you?" Curry paused to light a

177

cigarette, then flicked the match into the fireplace. "I wanted to talk to Ackerman privately to see if he wanted to buy Dwyer's stable and I didn't want Dwyer to know. Lew agreed to stop by."

"Why didn't you tell the police?" asked Charlie. He glanced at Krause who had his hands shoved into the pockets of his brown suit coat and stood almost motionless, as if waiting to be clicked on.

"I still didn't want Dwyer to know and it didn't seem very important."

"Why didn't you want Dwyer to know?"

Curry was wearing jeans and a blue and white gingham shirt with pearl snaps. The shirt fit him tightly, exposing ridges of muscle across his stomach. His short copper-colored hair looked like it had been brushed moments before.

"He's signed the stable over to his daughter, my wife," Curry said. "I'm running the place and legally we're owners. We wouldn't sell it while he was alive, but I thought it would do no harm to see if Lew was interested."

"Why did Dwyer try to kill himself?"

"I told you, he's a sick man. Lew's death upset him, but he's been depressed for a long time now."

"You didn't put anything in his food, did you?" asked Charlie.

Curry drew one last puff on his cigarette and tossed it in the fireplace. "What do you mean by that?" he asked.

Glancing down, Charlie saw that Curry was standing on one of his best white shirts. "Did Dwyer guess you'd killed Ackerman?" he asked. "Is that why he took the pills?"

"Why should I kill Ackerman?"

"Because Neal Claremon told him you were going to burn Dwyer's stable for the insurance money so you could build a big hotel on the property. That's also why you killed Claremon. Somehow he found out you were planning a fire

178

and you wanted him dead. So tell me, what did you and Ackerman really talk about?"

Curry glanced down, saw Charlie's shirt and pushed it aside with the point of his black cowboy boot. He seemed unconcerned by Charlie's accusation. "You really expect me to confess to a murder?" he said.

Charlie didn't answer this but kept staring at Curry as if he were waiting. He was irritated at himself for not picking up his clothes and felt it weakened his credibility.

Curry took a quick look at Krause, then shrugged. "I didn't think I had any choice," he said. "Ackerman told me if there was a fire he'd go to the police."

"And so you shot him?"

Curry lit another cigarette. This time he watched the match burn a little before blowing it out. "I knew when he swam and I knew the layout of the Y. It seemed easy."

Charlie couldn't imagine why Curry had decided to confess. In a way, Charlie was sorry he had, because now he couldn't think what to do with him. He didn't believe Curry would allow him to call Peterson to come and arrest him. Thinking about the next few minutes, he couldn't guess how they would turn out; and as he ran through the possibilities, he became more nervous. Also, in the back of his mind, something else had begun to bother him. It was like an itch beginning to declare itself.

"And you tried to kill me and Victor too, right? You knocked us off the road."

Before Curry could answer, Krause took his hands from his pockets and began walking slowly toward Curry who was about eight feet away. Curry looked at him but did no more than toss away his cigarette.

"Jack," said Charlie, "leave him alone."

As Krause walked, he reached under his coat and Charlie knew he was reaching for his revolver.

"Krause, you can't do it!" Charlie took a few steps toward him and stopped.

Krause paused to glance at Charlie and in that moment Curry moved forward and as easily as a dancer raised his left leg and whipped it toward Krause's stomach, burying his boot, it seemed, in the fat. Krause was thrown back, grabbing at his stomach and retching. He tripped over a chair and sprawled backward across the dining room table, which creaked, then one of its legs buckled under and Krause was sent crashing to the floor.

Fumbling at his waist, Charlie drew his revolver and pointed it at Curry. "Stand right where you are."

Curry looked as if nothing had happened. Krause rolled over on his stomach, then pushed himself up on his hands and knees and knelt there gagging and coughing.

Then Charlie heard a noise behind him. As he began to turn, he realized that what had been bothering him was whether the kitchen door had been locked or if only the screen had been latched. Before he could even complete this thought, an arm wrapped itself around his throat and he was yanked backward. Then a damp cloth was pressed against his mouth. The cloth reeked of chloroform and Charlie told himself he had to act quickly. It was the last thing he remembered.

21

WHEN CHARLIE RETURNED from New York City
after his ill-fated search for the missing son of a high school
sweetheart and told his wife he wanted a divorce, her response was one of fierce indignation. As a no-nonsense
business woman, she had always seen herself as the long-
suffering member of the Charlie Bradshaw and Marge Odel
Bradshaw team, while Charlie, with his passion for criminal
history, Little League baseball, and the aquatic films of
Esther Williams, accounted, she thought, for a lot of non-
sense. Still, by being his wife she had located herself in the
same family as her older sister who had married Charlie's
middle cousin, Robert; and although Charlie, unlike Robert,
was no pillar of society, he was at least a sergeant in the
police department and people, for no reason she could
imagine, appeared to respect him.

Marge found it difficult to believe that Charlie was leaving
her for what she called no reason. There was no other
woman and while they hadn't been doing much talking,
neither had they been quarreling. They had been sitting
in Lou's Luncheonette on Broadway across from the Montana Bookstore and Charlie had told her, "I just don't feel
like being married anymore."

"Feel like," Marge had said, "what do you think I've felt like being married fifteen years to a simpleton?"

Charlie had never thought of himself as a simpleton and so was surprised rather than hurt. He imagined simpletons as being clownish and ineffectual. People whose shoes were always untied and had wisps of straw caught in their hair. But since that time whenever he did something that turned out unhappily, the word would reoccur to him and he would ask himself if Marge hadn't been right.

It was the word "simpleton" which kept repeating itself in Charlie's brain when he woke to find himself lying uncomfortably on his stomach on a floor covered with dirty straw. As he tried to get up, he realized a thick rope was wound loosely around and around his body. His head felt heavy, as if it were several sizes larger; and beyond aching miserably, it pulsed like a blinking light. He shut his eyes and thought of Marge. When he opened them again and glanced around he saw Krause, wound as he was with a thick rope, lying unconscious a few feet away. Noticing the wooden walls, Dutch door, the one bare light bulb dangling from a wire, mounds of soiled straw, Charlie realized they were in a horse stall, but how they got there he had no idea. Mixed with the smell of horse and manure was another smell which he at first couldn't place. Then he recognized it as gasoline. As he began to think about this, he heard a noise behind him.

Kicking his feet and flopping onto his side, Charlie turned himself enough to see Wayne Curry standing near the door of the stall. Around Curry were ten five-gallon gasoline cans. Curry looked at him as if he weren't there at all, as if he were just so much more dirty straw. It was at that point Charlie realized that Curry not only intended to burn the stable, he meant to burn him and Krause along with it. The shock of this stirred him into speech.

182

"You really think you can get away with it?" A residue of chloroform made his tongue feel heavy and he spoke sleepily.

Curry didn't answer. The mixture of gasoline and manure smelled so strong that Charlie was afraid he was going to be sick and he found himself concentrating on the silver horse-head buckle of Curry's belt in order to control his increasing nausea.

"Won't they be suspicious when they find our bodies?" he asked. Charlie tried to keep his voice steady and conversational, as if he found nothing unusual about the present situation. Part of this was pride, part was the concern that if he acknowledged his fear it would overwhelm him.

Curry lifted two of the five-gallon cans, began to leave, then looked back at Charlie. "You went to a number of bars the other day looking for a man who is generally known as a professional torch. That wasn't very smart of you, Bradshaw. You get found here, what do you guess people will think?" Curry turned back toward the door, kicked it open with his boot and left.

As Charlie lay on the straw testing the ropes, he tried to answer Curry's question. Even though witnesses could be found to testify he had been looking for the torch, he couldn't believe Peterson would accept this as sufficient evidence of his guilt. But as he thought that, he realized why Curry had talked to Field, Peterson, his cousin, and presumably others to complain about Charlie's supposed harassment. If Curry could make people think Charlie had a grudge against him, then perhaps he could also make them think he had set the stable on fire.

Immediately, Charlie pushed the thought away. People would never believe it. But what was his reputation in Saratoga? Unstable and undependable. It was known that he and Krause had been badly disturbed by Ackerman's death,

183

that Charlie had tried to investigate the murder himself and had come to believe that Dwyer and/or Curry were responsible. The people who would know him to be innocent were not people of power. Again Charlie thought of the word "simpleton."

In any case, Charlie knew, his body would be found along with Krause's. A little more chloroform, remove the ropes, and blow them up. In his years as a policeman, Charlie had come across would-be arsonists who had blown themselves up by lighting a cigarette or even striking a nail with the heal of a shoe at the wrong moment. Certainly, people would think it improbable he had burned down Dwyer's stable, but then, to contradict it, here was his body in evidence.

Charlie began to pull frantically at the ropes, then he forced himself to relax. His fear kept rising up as a palpable object and he had to keep clenching himself to push it away. All the intellectualizing and analyzing wouldn't change the fact that he was tied up on the floor of a horse stall which would soon be on fire. Charlie looked at Krause, saw he was still unconscious, and decided that one way or another he had to get over to him.

The door opened and Curry reappeared and picked up two more gas cans. Charlie tried to heave himself into a sitting position but couldn't and flopped back down. As Curry started to leave, Charlie said, "Peterson won't believe it."

Curry stopped with his back to Charlie and turned his head slightly. "Peterson's my friend. We're supposed to play golf tomorrow afternoon. He'll believe what I want him to believe."

The door opened and a young man whom Charlie recognized as a groom he had seen several days before came in and picked up two more gas cans.

"You got those rags in place?"

184

"Frank's hooking them up to the house." The man looked at Charlie, then looked away. He had curly black hair and wore jeans and a black T-shirt with the name "Santana" printed across the front in red lettering.

"And the shed rows?"

"Just finished. I'm going to douse 'em again now. You going to leave these last four cans in here?"

"That's right," said Curry. "Bradshaw needs help burning. He's too green."

"Maybe I should pour some over his clothes?"

"That's okay. This twenty gallons should do it. Right, Bradshaw?"

When Charlie didn't answer, Curry shrugged, then he and the groom left the stall. In the long run, Charlie knew it wouldn't work. Curry didn't realize how much Charlie had found out, how he had involved all his guards, had discovered a motive for burning the stable and a personality reckless enough to try it. Eventually Curry might go to trial, but Charlie wouldn't be alive to testify.

He thought again of Claremon's statement that there was nothing worse than a stable fire. Here, one day before the opening of the meet, the stable was at its fullest and most valuable. Grooms were probably away at the movies or a bar or the clubhouse. Perhaps there weren't even any grooms staying here. Curry's guard would be found knocked out. Charlie had seen fifty gallons of gasoline and there was probably more. With all that wood and straw, it would take only a couple of minutes for the building to be totally engulfed in fire, while the trailers of gasoline-soaked rags would carry the fire to the other buildings. He thought of the horses crazy with fear and his own death which would at least, he thought, be fairly quick.

Again Charlie tried to switch off that part of his mind which was trying to distance himself from his present pre-

185

dicament by turning it into an analytical problem. The ropes were loose and he guessed that had been done so they wouldn't leave marks on their bodies. He looked around the stall for any sharp object, any nail sticking out of the wall or even a rusty pipe, but the stall was empty. His revolver was gone, as was his small Swiss army knife.

Looking toward Krause, Charlie saw he had begun to stir. Still on his stomach, Charlie began to half push and half wriggle his way toward him. As he inched his way along, he could feel damp straw being pushed down the collar of his shirt.

Krause raised his head, looked around, then let his head fall back on the straw. Pushing himself forward another foot, Charlie bumped his head against Krause's shoulder, stirring him awake again.

"Krause, come on, we've got to get out of here."

"I can't move, Charlie."

Like Charlie's, Krause's hands were tied behind him. Charlie pushed himself forward, then heaved himself over until his back was facing Krause. "Can you reach any of these knots?" he asked.

After a pause, Krause said, "Maybe with my teeth. Try and get closer."

Charlie heaved himself back a little further. "Now?"

"A bit more."

Again Charlie heaved himself back. This time he felt his hands bump against Krause. There was a tug, then another as Krause's teeth pulled against the knots.

The door opened and Curry came back in. Seeing what Charlie and Krause were doing, he took a step forward, then stopped. He watched the two of them as if they were some slightly interesting experiment. Then Krause grew aware of his presence and lifted his head.

"Just like something out of an old movie," said Curry. He walked quickly toward Charlie, drew back a boot and kicked him hard in the stomach so he was thrown back against Krause. Charlie gagged and tried to curl himself into a ball. Curry reached down, grabbed hold of the ropes, and dragged Charlie back across the stall so his face scraped on the floor. Then he dropped him. As Charlie rolled away and tried to catch his breath, Curry kicked him again.

"It's going to give me pleasure to see you burn, Bradshaw. You been getting in my way all week. The world's full of jerks like you: no class, no money, and no brains. Well, I'm going to roast you."

As Curry turned toward the door, he stumbled against one of the four remaining gas cans, knocking it over. The top was loose and popped off and immediately gasoline began to gurgle onto the straw several feet away from where Charlie was lying.

Curry looked at it but left it where it was. Then he glanced toward Charlie and began to smile, showing his teeth. Charlie stared back at him, trying to keep his face from showing fear. After a moment, Curry turned and left the stall.

"You all right, Charlie?" asked Krause.

"Yeah, let's try it again." Rolling over on his stomach, Charlie began to wriggle and push and heave his way toward Krause. The pain in his stomach and side where Curry had kicked him was almost a distraction from his fear. He wondered if Curry had cracked a rib and what the coroner would think when he discovered the broken rib at the inquest. Then he wondered if it was brave of him to be thinking of his own inquest, instead of dissolving into terror. Then he again thought of the word "simpleton."

When Charlie had pushed himself about five feet toward

187

Krause, he heard the door open behind him. He let his head drop forward on the straw. He felt futile and wished everything were over.

For a moment the stall was quiet, then a voice said, "Whatcha doin down there, playing caterpillar?"

Charlie yanked his head around to see Victor standing in the doorway with Ackerman's small-bore pump gun in the crook of his right arm. His left arm, still in its cast, was supported by a sling made from two blue bandannas.

"Hurry," said Charlie, "get us out of these ropes. No jokes, Victor."

"Vic." Victor laid the shotgun down on the straw, took a small penknife from the pocket of his jeans, and began sawing through the ropes which bound Charlie's hands.

"You bring the police?" asked Charlie. He could hardly believe Victor was really there and he kept turning his head to make sure.

"Nah, I just came over with Rico and Phil. When you didn't come back, we decided to go over to your house. It reeked of chloroform so after I called the Backstretch and some other places we decided to take a peek over here. What's going on?"

Charlie scrambled to his feet and grabbed the shotgun. "Curry wants to burn us up with the stable. Are Rico and Phil armed?"

"Nope, I decided to bring along the shotgun at the last minute." He began to cut the ropes from Krause.

"You ever fired one?" asked Charlie, keeping the gun pointed toward the door.

"Never had the opportunity. Rico wanted to carry it, but he's still on pro so I figured I better carry it myself being the oldest and most responsible. He put some bullets in it for me."

"Shells," said Krause.

188

"That's what I said," said Victor.

"How're you going to shoot it with only one arm?"

"All's I need is one finger," said Victor.

Krause looked at him, started to speak, then embraced him instead, lifting Victor's feet off the floor and squeezing him until he made a squeaking noise. "Thanks," said Krause, setting him back down.

Victor straightened his gray sweat shirt. "Nada, like the Ricans say," he said.

"You seen Curry?" asked Charlie.

"Yeah, I seen him and a coupla his buddies prowling around with gasoline cans."

"Where's Rico and Phil?"

"Dunno, we split up. They were goin to check the other buildings."

Charlie hefted the shotgun in his hands. He guessed it held five shells. He had used a .410 several times as a kid and had never hit anything except a squirrel which he'd wounded and then had to nurse back to health. He seemed to recall that its effective range was under twenty-five yards. He wondered if he had time to get to a telephone. Then he heard a gunshot. After a moment, he heard another. Charlie took a deep breath, then let it out slowly so it made a whistling noise. Whatever was happening, they would have to deal with it themselves.

"Let's go," said Charlie. He flicked off the light and opened the door.

Charlie didn't know what kind of scene he expected to find on the other side of the door, but he at least assumed it would be violent. Instead it was bucolic: a full moon lighting up the elms and the shed rows, outlining the mansard roof of the two-story house at the center of the stable complex. There was no one in sight and no sound except for an occasional whinny. They had been in a small equipment barn

189

between the training track and the house. On either side the four shed rows stretched away in the moonlight. Linking the barn to the house and stables were ghostly trails of white rags and sheets smelling of gasoline. One passed near Charlie. He hurried over and began to kick it apart.

There was a third shot and Charlie dropped to his knees. Then he saw someone running from the shed row at the farthest left toward the house. The man must have seen them at the same time, because he stopped and pointed his arm at them. There was a spark of light, then a gunshot.

"Get down," shouted Charlie.

He was aware of Krause and Victor crouching down behind him. Charlie flopped onto his stomach in the grass, aimed the shotgun at the man near the house, and fired. At that range he didn't expect the birdshot to have any effect, but it would at least make the man keep his distance.

The man backed toward the house and fired again. Charlie heard a thunk as the bullet hit the wall of the barn behind him. Since he was still in a direct line with the barn, he was afraid that a ricochet off one of the metal gas cans might cause a spark which could ignite the gasoline-soaked straw. He crawled toward the house and fired again. Then, from the shed row to his left, came more gunshots and he knew someone was attempting to ignite the barn.

Turning, Charlie saw Victor and Krause crawling on their bellies toward several elm trees to their right. Charlie knew he should be breaking up the other trailers of rags. Instead he tried to make himself as flat as possible. He felt powerless with the small shotgun. He fired at the shed row to his left, then he saw what he had been most afraid of: a snaking quick movement of flame racing along the rope of sheets and rags toward the small barn. If the barn went up, the other trailers would be ignited.

Charlie jumped to his feet. "Get those trailers," he

shouted. "Krause, Victor, break up those lines of rags."

There were more gunshots and Charlie heard the bullets hit the wall of the barn. The flame on the line of rags dashed along the ground like a small angry animal. Then it rushed into the barn. For a moment, there was silence, then the barn exploded, sending a flash of orange flame through the doorway with a great whoosh.

Even as the barn became engulfed in fire and burning debris shot into the air around them, Charlie was running toward the two trailers extending to the shed rows to his right. Glancing over his shoulder, he saw both trailers burning, seeming to rush along the ground faster than he could hope to run. He reached the first line of rags and hurriedly kicked it apart. Then he ran toward the second about five yards away. As the flame snaked along the ground, Charlie knew he wouldn't be able to reach it in time. Raising the shotgun, he fired and the birdshot struck the string of rags, scattering them. The rushing flame flickered to a stop. Even though he had only been about two yards away and the shot had been simple, Charlie immediately wanted to tell someone about it.

"The house," shouted Victor. "Get the one to the house!"

Turning, Charlie saw Krause running toward the house while in a converging line was a white length of sheets and rags with an orange flame skittering along it. Charlie also began to run toward it, although he was farther away. The burning barn behind them lit up the yard and the air was thick with smoke. About ten yards away to his right, Charlie saw the form of Phil Tyler lying motionless in the dirt with one arm thrown up above his head. Then there were more gunshots: these coming from the house. Krause had nearly reached the string of sheets, but as the gun started firing from the front window he dove to the ground and the fire on the trailer sputtered past him, sputtered up the front walk, sputtered up the steps and into the house. Charlie, who had also ducked down, jumped to his feet and ran toward Phil Tyler. There were the sounds of cracking, burning wood and horses whinnying in terror. Then, added to that, was another great whoosh and the sound of glass breaking as the house exploded in fire and orange flames smashed through the downstairs front windows.

Seconds later a man came rushing out of the house with his clothing on fire. He half fell, half jumped from the steps and stumbled into the yard. He still had his gun and was firing as he ran, but randomly, up in the air, wherever the gun happened to be pointing as if the act of firing could drive away the fire that engulfed him.

He was about twenty yards away and Charlie left Tyler and ran toward him. Flames were shooting up the side of the house and now he could see them upstairs as well. There was another whoosh and the second-floor windows blew out, sending pieces of glass spraying across the yard. Victor shouted something, but the noise of the fire and terrified screaming of the horses was so great that his words were lost in the roar. Both Victor and Krause were running toward the burning man, while beyond him toward the further shed rows Charlie saw Rico also running. Rico ran with one hand held out and Charlie realized he was holding a gun.

The burning man slowed to a stop and stood swaying back and forth still wrapped in flame. He stood beneath one of the large elms, and the flames threw light and shadow on the trunk, while the leaves above him flickered as if in a wind. The man raised his arms high above his head and began to cry out in a wailing voice that seemed to rise above the sound of the fire. It was at that moment that Krause reached him. Without pausing, Krause tackled him, knocking the man to the ground and rolling him over in the dirt. Victor followed, tossing dirt on the flames, patting

192

out the small fires that sprang up on Krause's clothing.

"It's not Curry," said Rico as he ran up to where Charlie stood. "I took care of one of the others with a bit of two-by-four."

"Find a phone," said Charlie. "There should be one in the shed rows. Get an ambulance and the fire department if they're not already on their way." Then, remembering Phil Tyler, he left Rico and ran back to him

Tyler was sprawled on his stomach with his feet wide apart. Bending over him, Charlie gently pushed his legs together, then turned him over. Tyler made a moaning noise. He had been shot in the shoulder and leg and was losing a lot of blood. The front of his white shirt was soaked red. Tyler slowly shook his head and opened his eyes.

"No more night duty, Charlie," he said. "I don't want to do no more night duty." Then he closed his eyes again.

Charlie heard sirens or thought he did. Looking up, he saw Victor standing beside him. His face seemed to flicker in the light from the burning house. He looked at Tyler and shook his head.

"I think that guy who was on fire is dead," said Victor. "Probably just as well. Anyway, I got his gun." He raised a .38 revolver and showed it to Charlie.

Charlie got to his feet. The gun looked like his own. He felt tired and his only gratification was that the horses were safe. "Is it loaded?" he asked.

"How can you tell?"

Charlie took it and flicked open the chamber. "It's empty." He checked his pockets for the extra shells but they were gone. Handing the revolver back to Victor, he knelt down to see if he could stop Tyler's bleeding.

Victor spun the revolver on his finger. "First a deadly weapon," he said. "Now a paperweight."

Rico ran up, then knelt beside Charlie. "Ambulance is

on its way." He tore open the fabric surrounding the bullet wound in Tyler's leg, then pressed his thumbs on a spot a little above the wound. "Doncha know any first aid?" he said. "Let me take care of this."

"What the fuck's Krause doin?" asked Victor, pointing to the parking lot about fifty yards away.

Charlie looked to see Krause yank open a car door, half disappear inside, then draw back and run to another car. In the middle of the lot was a large mercury vapor light on a telephone pole and surrounding it were about eight cars and several pickup trucks. Krause yanked open another car door, half disappeared, then left the car and ran to another.

"Wacko," said Victor, shoving the empty revolver in his back pocket. "Always happens to boxers sooner or later."

Krause was now at the door of a red pickup truck. This time he climbed in entirely. There was the sound of the starter, then the motor caught and the lights went on. Almost without thinking, Charlie found himself running toward the lot. Victor was only a little behind him.

"Where's your car?" Charlie shouted.

"We came in Rico's. It's parked on the road. I got the keys."

The pickup bumped out of the parking lot, swung toward the front gates about two hundred yards away, and accelerated. Caught in the headlights halfway up the metal gate was the figure of a man. The person reached the top of the gate, then disappeared.

"It's Curry," shouted Victor. "There was another car parked further up the road."

When the red pickup reached the gate, it barely paused as it smashed through the tall metal panels, sending them flying back. Charlie ran faster. He was still holding the pump gun in his right hand.

194

22

APPARENTLY the blue Plymouth Fury had missed the curve on the Avenue of Pines, bumped over the curb, and slid sideways into the big spruce in the center of the grass triangle. In any case, the car was a mess.

The Avenue of Pines ran between Dwyer's stable and downtown Saratoga, bordering the Saratoga Spa State Park and the Performing Arts Center. Charlie usually avoided it in the summer because it was crowded with tourists, but this night—or rather morning, since it was nearly 2:00 A.M.—the road was deserted.

The blue Fury seemed halfway up the spruce and what had been an expensively sculptured front end now appeared to be mimicking a concertina. The front and rear windows had been smashed while the back end with its elaborate stabilizer had been turned into so much scrap metal, presumably where Krause's pickup truck had rammed into it. Then there were additional gouge marks in the grass where the pickup had backed up and taken off toward the rear gates of the Performing Arts Center less than a quarter of a mile away.

Victor got back into Rico's tan Ford. "Nobody's there and there's no blood. Either he's okay or he's a vampire."

Charlie backed up, turned, then bumped the Ford over

the curb as he followed the tracks of the pickup toward the theater.

"Why would he go in there?" asked Victor. He had one hand pressed against the dashboard and was pushing himself back in his seat.

"He's probably cutting through to the other side. If he can get to Route 50, then he can stop a car at the light. Except for the fences, this is the shortest way across."

"And what's Krause doin, if you're so smart?"

"Krause wants to kill him."

The large metal gates onto the grounds of the amphitheater had been smashed open and ripped from their hinges. Charlie drove through the gates and stopped near a pair of green trash cans that lay on their sides dented like beer cans. Ten feet further on the red pickup was caught up on a stone bench and tilted so far to the right that it seemed ready to topple over. Its lights were on and shone up into the leaves of the elms. There were three bullet holes in the smashed front window, but no sign of blood. As Victor and Charlie stood by the truck, they heard sirens. A moment later, there was a gunshot from the direction of the theater. It was a small noise like a distant backfire. Charlie turned toward it. The theater was a huge fan-shaped building which could seat more than five thousand persons and provided space for another seven thousand on the sloping lawns. Although roofed, the sides were open and on very windy, rainy nights only the large balcony would stay completely dry. There was another gunshot followed immediately by its echo. Charlie was certain it came from the theater.

"Let's go," he said. Still holding the shotgun, he began running toward the side of the theater, aiming down toward the stage which in a few days would be ready for the Phila-

196

delphia Orchestra now that the New York City Ballet had completed its season.

The full moon was bright enough, Charlie thought, to allow him to read a book, and he and Victor had no trouble making their way between the small trees and bushes along the side of the theater. The theater itself, however, was dark except for the red exit signs. Charlie and Victor ducked down between the first row and the orchestra pit as they peered back into the massive black space looking for some sign of Curry or Krause. Some birds in the theater had been disturbed and were twittering wildly. The sirens seemed much nearer and Charlie guessed that the police had found Curry's wrecked Plymouth Fury.

There was a metallic noise as of something hitting the back of one of the seats. This was followed by a spark and a gunshot, then the whine of a ricochet. The spark seemed to occur high up in the air and Charlie guessed that Curry was standing near the railing of the balcony. More birds began to twitter frantically and the air seemed full of the whirr of wings. Charlie raised the shotgun, pointed it toward the balcony, and fired. The explosion was immense as it echoed through the black space. Then there was a rattling noise as the birdshot fell among the seats, far short of where Curry presumably was standing. Seconds later, there were three more gunshots which pinged and ricocheted off the seats around them and sent Charlie and Victor diving to the floor.

"Give me some more shells," said Charlie.

"I didn't bring any more. How'd I know you'd turn into a shootin fool?"

There were two more gunshots and the bullets clanged into the metal chairs and music stands in the orchestra pit. It would give, Charlie thought, some oboist something interesting to talk about.

"What'd you want to shoot at him for in the first place?" asked Victor. "You only made him mad."

"I want to distract him from Krause."

"He's probably already killed Krause."

Charlie crawled along the concrete floor with the empty shotgun balanced across his arms until he found the gap of an aisle. From where he lay, he could see straight back to a red exit sign at the rear of the theater. The birds were still chirping and fluttering through the dark. Charlie guessed Krause was also on the balcony and felt the best he could do was to keep Curry's attention on himself and so give Krause his chance. Getting to his feet, he ran about twenty yards up the aisle, then ducked down again.

"Curry," he shouted. "Throw down your gun. I'm going to take you to jail." Even as he said this, Charlie knew he was using nearly the same words Wyatt Earp had used when he arrested Ben Thompson for shooting down the sheriff of Ellsworth, Kansas.

Before his words had stopped echoing, there were two more gunshots, both of which hit the seat just above him. Charlie lay on his back and looked up into the dark. As if it were a film being shown on the roof of the theater, he pictured the burning house and the man wrapped in flame leaping from the front steps. Then Charlie took a deep breath, rolled over, and got to his feet. Through the back of the theater he could see car lights bumping across the grass: three sets of lights with a blue flashing gumball on the top of each car.

Charlie took the shotgun by the barrel, swung it around and around his head, then let go. There was a silence, then a crash, followed by another as the shotgun bounced across the seats in front of him. Immediately, there were two more gunshots.

Charlie heard a noise behind him and turned to see

Victor sitting in the aisle. "If he ever gets a look at you," said Victor, "he's goin to turn you into a fuckin sieve. I don't see whatcha want to drive him crazy for. I'm sick of stayin down here under the chewing gum."

Just as he stopped speaking, the lights went on in the theater. Charlie ducked behind the seats. Looking up, he saw Curry standing as if frozen by the railing near the middle of the balcony. He held his pistol with both hands and was pointing it down into the theater. To his left at a side entrance, Charlie saw Chief Peterson standing with about six policemen. One of them pointed up at the balcony.

"Jesus," said Victor, "look at Krause."

The ex-boxer was crouched down about ten feet behind Curry. As Charlie looked, Krause jumped to his feet and began to run down the aisle toward Curry.

Peterson stepped forward into the theater. He was holding a revolver. "Krause," he shouted, "stop or I'll shoot."

The only person to respond was Curry, who spun around and saw Krause only several feet away. Dodging to his right, Curry raised his gun and fired twice. Krause staggered, but then reached Curry, knocked aside his gun and, grabbing him by his belt and arm, lifted him up until he held him at shoulder height nearly forty feet above the main floor.

"Put him down," shouted Peterson. "Krause, I'm . . . ."

Krause stood swaying at the railing. His brown suit was torn and flecked with straw. He tried to raise Curry even higher above his head, lift him until his arms were stretched straight up, but Curry kept kicking and clawing at his face.

Slowly, Krause tilted against the railing, tilted more until almost gently his body tilted over the side and his feet kicked upward as he fell off the balcony. Charlie was already running toward the spot where they would hit. As the two men fell, Krause pushed Curry away. Curry began to scream, a sharp staccato scream which he repeated over and over. Then there was a thud and crash as they hit the floor. Krause fell into aisle, Curry among the seats.

Charlie was the first one to reach them. Curry lay folded up between the two back rows. His head was twisted nearly all the way around and it was clear that his neck must have hit the back of a seat, snapping it, and killing him instantly. His eyes were open and his face had the same blank expression it had had in life. Charlie turned away to where Krause lay on his back. His eyes were also open, but he was alive and staring at the ceiling. Blood was trickling from the corners of his mouth. Charlie knelt down beside him.

Krause lifted one of his big hands and slowly began brushing bits of straw from the lapels of his suit coat. "Charlie," he asked, "is Curry dead?"

Charlie nodded and began stroking his friend's forehead.

"Never killed a man before," said Krause. He spoke quietly as if he were forcing the words to come a long distance. "Makes me feel good," he said.

"Don't talk any more," said Charlie. He was aware of Victor standing beside him. Various Saratoga policemen were rushing around. Peterson had been looking at Curry. Now he joined Charlie and Victor.

"Everything's all right now, isn't it, Charlie?" asked Krause. "I mean, I did the right thing."

"You did fine," said Charlie.

"I think I'll rest a little," said Krause.

As Charlie got to his feet, Peterson grabbed his arm and pulled him toward him, digging his fingers into Charlie's muscle. Then he jabbed a revolver in Charlie's stomach.

"If he lives," said Peterson, "I'm going to see he's sent away forever. You too, Bradshaw. You'll be away from Saratoga for a long time."

Charlie looked down at the revolver pressing against his

200

stomach. Peterson's face was bright red. Slowly, Charlie raised his hand until it touched Peterson's cheek. For a moment, he thought of Krause's story about the sportswriter he had always regretted not hitting. Then Charlie patted the police chief's face.

"Peterson," he said, "you were always a stupid man."

23

NORMALLY, downtown Saratoga at 7:30 Sunday morning was a pretty dull place. But this morning, July 30, just a day before the opening of the track there were horse trailers, campers, Winnebagos, grooms in souped-up Fords; exercise boys, trainers, jockeys and their agents, bug boys going in and out of Lou's Luncheonette or the 24-hour Star Market, and enough general activity that the mere sight of it was enough to tire Victor out.

It was a blue, cloudless morning and the breeze blowing down Broadway carried bits of paper, styrofoam cups, paper bags so that even the street seemed in a hurry. Victor braked slightly as the front page of the *Racing Form* blew across the windshield of his Dodge Dart. He and Charlie were driving along Broadway toward the Spa City Diner where they intended to have breakfast. In his mind, Victor was debating between poached eggs, French toast, or both. He was most inclined to both. He hadn't slept, his eyes felt scratchy and his last meal was a distant memory: a vague cheeseburger and maybe a small slice of apple pie. They had only just left police headquarters after spending hours talking and waiting around, talking and waiting around. At the same time, Victor was surprised to be at liberty at all. Back at the Performing Arts Center, he had decided he was in for a ten-year jail term and he'd worried how to break the news to his son in Chicago.

It was Charlie who got them out of that. After he had patted Peterson's cheek, he suggested the police chief examine Curry's fancy European pistol—a 15-shot Beretta Model 92S-1—to see if it wasn't the same gun which killed Ackerman and Claremon. Then he suggested that Peterson check the front fender of the red pickup from Dwyer's stable for traces of yellow paint from Charlie's Volkswagen. After that he suggested they return to Dwyer's stable to question the man whom Rico had captured. Despite this, Peterson still insisted on arresting them, although even his own men were apologetic.

Curry was dead, as was the other man who had been burned: Victor never learned his name. Peterson had found the second accomplice—Harry Something—bound hand and foot in Dwyer's parking lot with Rico standing nearby with a length of two-by-four. Rico had already convinced Harry that the world would be a happier place if he told all. Driving down Broadway, Victor took pleasure in remembering Peterson's face as Harry explained how Curry intended to burn the stable, where he bought the gasoline, how he meant to frame Charlie and Krause and have them killed in the fire.

After that Peterson grudgingly admitted he must have been mistaken and they drove to police headquarters, where much of the night was spent with Charlie and Victor giving their statements. They had sat in Peterson's large office and Victor went so far as to smoke one of Peterson's expensive cigars, even though he didn't like cigars. Peterson had listened and at least had the decency not to interrupt. Subdued was how Victor described him. Then, around seven, the State Police called to say that Curry's Beretta was indeed the same gun that killed Ackerman and Claremon, while the red pickup was the one that bumped Charlie into the lake.

Phil Tyler was in critical condition but would recover. With Krause it wasn't so certain. Not only had bones been broken in his fall from the balcony, but he had been shot once in the abdomen. When Victor and Charlie left the police station for the Spa City Diner, the doctors were pessimistic. Charlie wanted to drive to the hospital after they had eaten and, although he would have preferred a dozen hours sleep in his own nice bed, Victor had agreed.

The car windows were open and as Victor drove he tapped his cast lightly against the steering wheel in time to the punk rock being broadcast by the Skidmore radio station. Charlie looked at him with mild irritation. He was worried about Tyler and Krause and kept telling himself if he had seen Peterson earlier both men would be all right. Even as he thought that, however, he doubted Peterson would have acted in time to save the stable.

Looking out at the bright summer morning, Charlie told himself he should feel glad it was nearly August, his favorite time of year. He told himself tomorrow he would take Doris Bailes to the track, and he would put some money on Red Fox in the fifth and maybe a whole new life would begin. Charlie kept repeating these things and after a while he told himself he felt a little better.

As they drove past the YMCA, Victor said, "What I don't see is why Curry shot Ackerman there instead of someplace else."

"Probably no place would have been easier," said Charlie. "He knew the Y and knew Krause usually stayed in the locker room."

"But what if Krause hadn't?" said Victor. "I mean, what if he had gone in with Ackerman?"

"I expect Curry was watching," said Charlie. "The weight

room is right by the locker room. He could have made sure Krause was in the locker room, then gone out the back and around to the side door of the pool."

"So if Krause had gone into the pool area, Curry would just of shot Ackerman some other time?"

Charlie yawned and covered his mouth. "I guess so," he said, "except he wanted to make it dramatic enough to look like a slick, cynical, professional killing."

"How come?"

"He wanted the murder blamed on organized crime, on racketeers who were angry at Ackerman for interfering with their gambling interests."

"And that's what Peterson did, right?"

"That's what he did at first," said Charlie. "I keep thinking he would have caught on eventually."

"Sure," said Victor, as he pulled into the lot of the Spa City Diner, "after you'd got burned up at the stable and I came pounding on his door. Dopes like Peterson can't figure anything unless it's written on a billboard. . . . By the way, you hear anything new about Dwyer?"

"No, he's still in a coma. The doctor said they'd just have to wait and see."

"You think Curry slipped him something?"

"I doubt it. I mean, I wouldn't put it past him, but more likely once Dwyer realized what was happening he decided to bow out. He didn't have the strength to fight Curry, much less stop him, and he couldn't have stood the publicity if Curry were arrested."

"Sounds like he was caught between the frying pan and the deep blue sea," said Victor, getting out of the car.

"That's about it," said Charlie.

The diner was attached to the bus station and despite the early hour large buses from New York and Montreal were disgorging tourists who hoped to make their fortune at the track. All over people were quarreling about cabs, buying tip sheets, being paranoid about their suitcases, and greeting old friends.

As Charlie made his way through the crowd and entered the restaurant, he thought it fortunate that his mother had quit her job as waitress to pursue her career as a racehorse owner. Charlie was dirty, his clothes were torn from being dragged around the stall, plus being spotted with soot and ash from the fire. Attempts to clean himself up at the police station had done little more than smear the dirt around. His mother would think such dishevelment indicated a night of carousing and she would remind him the family had a position to maintain, that it was Charlie's duty to look what she called his picture-pleasing best.

They took a table in the new part of the diner and the waitress brought them coffee. It was a large room filled with clattering plates, harried waitresses, and customers who all wanted something more. Charlie glanced around, then picked up his menu.

"You know," said Victor, "I partly came to Saratoga because I no longer felt safe in the city, but in the past week my arm's been broke, I was nearly drowned, and I've been shot at, I don't know how many times, a lot. If in the city I'd gone out on First Avenue and shouted, 'Ricans, take me, I'm yours,' I couldn't have had it any worse."

Charlie closed his menu and sipped his coffee. He didn't want Victor to leave. "So you're going back?" he asked.

Victor shrugged. "Like I say, it beats watchin the TV. Maybe I'll stay a bit longer." Taking a handful of napkins, Victor blew his nose. Then he scratched under his arm, leaned back in his chair, and glanced around the room looking for cute girls. After a moment, he said, "By the way, you know those three guys at that table over there? They keep starin at you."

206

Charlie glanced in the direction Victor indicated and saw his three cousins just finishing breakfast. They were clean, prosperous, and obviously respectable. All the dirt on Charlie's body suddenly felt heavy. He gave a half-hearted wave, then watched as the three men ignored it and returned to their meal.

"They're my cousins," said Charlie. "I was pretty much brought up with them."

"Guess they don't like the straw in your hair," said Victor.

Charlie again picked up his menu and tried to decide if he really wanted blueberry pancakes. Then he gave it up. He wondered what new round of gossip he would have to contend with. In the long run, it would be easier to go bad. But as he thought this, Charlie grew irritated at himself for being so easily cowed. Hadn't he outwitted the police? Hadn't he solved Ackerman's murder? Charlie pushed away his menu. He would force his cousins to acknowledge him. No more would he stand for their moral bullying.

"There," said Victor, "that got them."

Charlie looked up to see his three cousins making their way between the crowded tables toward the exit. They seemed to wobble with indignation.

"What'd you do?" asked Charlie.

"Blew 'em a kiss," said Victor.

Ross Macdonald "carried form and style about as far as they would go, writing classic family tragedies in the guise of private detective mysteries" – *The Guardian*

"Without in the least abating my admiration for Dashiell Hammett or Raymond Chandler, I should like to venture the heretical suggestion that Ross Macdonald is a better novelist than either of them" – Anthony Boucher, *New York Times Book Review*

"The finest detective novels ever written by an American" – William Goldman, *New York Times Book Review*

BLACK MONEY
Ross Macdonald

Almost anything can happen in Montevista, where the rich and the bored and the ambitious have their playground. So when Lew Archer is hired by a melancholy, overweight young millionaire to rescue his beautiful fiancee from the clutches of a self-styled French aristocrat, he sighs and takes it in his stride. But finding out just who Francis Martel really is leads Archer to the bitter heart of a Californian family tragedy, and into a world of shady money, sexual intrigue and cold-blooded murder.

THE BLUE HAMMER
Ross Macdonald

Finding Ruth Biemeyer's stolen painting looks simple enough, but the case keeps sliding off into other cases, other people's lives. Across two states and thirty years, through a world where money still buys silence, to a missing painter and a double murder, and the subterranean jolt as a dead man is thrown out of his grave.

THE MOVING TARGET
Ross Macdonald

A lot of people would go to a lot of trouble to get their hands on $100,000 in small notes. Kidnapping, for instance. And that's how it looks to Lew Archer when he's hired to trace a missing billionaire. But five murders later and with a tightening circle of suspects, $100,000 no longer seems an adequate reason for all that trouble.

FINDERS WEEPERS
Max Byrd

It all started when Leo Matz hired Mike Haller to find a prostitute who'd been left $800,000. Within hours of taking the case Haller is framed for a shooting he didn't do and his PI licence has been revoked. But whoever fixed the frame-up has misjudged Haller badly, and that will cost him and a lot of other people dear.

"In the first rank of American crime writing" – *The Times*

"All we remember as best from Hammett, Chandler and Macdonald" – *New Republic*

"Thrillers don't come much better crafted or written than Byrd's" – *Time Out*

Brown's Requiem
James Ellroy

Fritz Brown runs a Private Detective agency as a tax dodge and makes his real money repossessing cars. That is until Freddy "Fat Dog" Baker – a golf caddy flashing a $7000 billfold – hires Brown to watch his beautiful sister and her elderly sugar daddy. From then on, Brown is plunged into the dark and violent underworld of a Californian lottery swindle that goes way back into the past.

"Finishes as strongly as the story engages" – *The Spectator*

"A strange but compelling read" – *Huddersfield Examiner*

Allison & Busby American Crime

ALWAYS A BODY TO TRADE
K.C. Constantine

Over the years Mario Balzic has built up a precarious balance between imperfect law and practicable order on the streets of Rocksburg, P.A. But now that balance is threatened: a zealous new major has been elected on a "law and order" ticket and a young woman has been gunned down in the street, victim of a professional hit.

"A marvellous writer . . . May Mario Balzic thrive!"
– *New York Times Book Review*

"K.C. Constantine – a pseudonym – writes like an angel: sharply and funnily, with an ear for dialogue that matches George V. Higgins . . . Balzic is undoubtedly the discovery of the moment"
– *The Times Literary Supplement*

FIVE LITTLE RICH GIRLS
Lawrence Block

Five Little Rich Girls is a witty, sexy, literate and dazzling pastiche of the great American mystery novel. Then suddenly it's also the real thing, for an overdose of heroin begins to look like murder, and Chip Harrison needs all the resources a seventeen-year-old can muster to get the information his eccentric boss, Leo Haig, needs to bring off a masterstroke of supersleuthing.

"His dialogue crackles like an overheard conversation in a New York bar"
– *Washington Post*

"Lovers alike of the American gumshoe novel and the Great Detective novel will be delighted by *Five Little Rich Girls*" – *Books & Bookmen*

Allison & Busby American Crime

THE HEAT'S ON
Chester Himes

The Heat's On is one of the fastest, funniest and hardest hitting thrillers Chester Himes ever wrote. From the start nothing goes right for ace black detectives, Coffin Ed Johnson and Grave Digger Jones. Try as they might, they always seem to be one hot step behind the cause of all the mayhem – three million dollars worth of heroin and a simple albino called Pinky.

"A crime writer of Chandlerian subtlety, though in a vein of sheer toughness very much his own" – *The Times*

"The books have lasting value – as thrillers, as streetwise documentaries, as chapters of black writing at its ribald and unaffected best. They are simply – or rather, not so simply, terrific" – *Sunday Times*

SARATOGA HEADHUNTER
Stephen Dobyns

Ex-cop Charlie Bradshaw's new career as a private detective is progressing so quietly his successful cousins try to persuade him he should take a job as a milkman. But then, one night Jimmy McClatchy turns up on his doorstep looking for a place to hide. And when Jimmy – a jockey who's turned State's Evidence in a Federal trial – winds up dead at Charlie's table, the reluctant detective's new career begins in earnest.

"Dick Francis had better look to his laurels. An American longshot appropriately named Dobyns, is coming up fast on the outside" – *Houston Post*

"His writing is honest, toughminded and as uncompromising as his unforgettable hero" – *Washington Post*

Allison & Busby American Crime

"Nobody tops Stark in his objective portrayals of a world of total amorality"
– *New York Times*

"A true existentialist . . . Parker conducts his business between the twin
worlds of organized crime and disorganzied society" – *City Limits*

THE MAN WITH THE GETAWAY FACE
Richard Stark

Outwitting the Syndicate means Parker must buy a new face. But once
the bandages are off, keeping the new identity secret becomes a
full-time occupation.

THE BLACK ICE SCORE
Richard Stark

Stealing the African's diamonds back from a museum in the heart of New
York appeals to the arch-pro in Parker, but the opposition's clumsy double-
cross brings out his mean streak.

THE JUGGER
Richard Stark

Jo Sheer was Parker's contact man. Now he's dead. But before he died he
talked, and what he knew could nail Parker to the wall with a hundred nails.

POINT BLANK
Richard Stark

Double-crossed, shot and left for dead in a burning house by his wife and his
one-time partner, Parker is out for revenge. He's also out for his share of the
take, and if that means taking on the Outfit, Parker doesn't care. He's owed
$45,000 and he's going to get it.

Allison & Busby American Crime

_____	**Five Little Rich Girls**	Lawrence Block	£2.95 pbk
_____	**The Topless Tulip Caper**	Lawrence Block	£2.95 pbk
_____	**California Thriller**	Max Byrd	£2.95 pbk
_____	**Finders Weepers**	Max Byrd	£2.95 pbk
_____	**Always A Body To Trade**	K.C. Constantine	£2.95 pbk
_____	**Saratoga Headhunter**	Stephen Dobyns	£2.95 pbk
_____	**Saratoga Swimmer**	Stephen Dobyns	£2.95 pbk
_____	**Brown's Requiem**	James Ellroy	£2.95 pbk
_____	**Blind Man with a Pistol**	Chester Himes	£2.95 pbk
_____	**The Heat's On**	Chester Himes	£2.95 pbk
_____	**Black Money**	Ross Macdonald	£2.95 pbk
_____	**The Blue Hammer**	Ross Macdonald	£2.95 pbk
_____	**The Moving Target**	Ross Macdonald	£3.50 pbk
_____	**Point Blank**	Richard Stark	£2.95 pbk
_____	**The Jugger**	Richard Stark	£2.95 pbk
_____	**The Black Ice Score**	Richard Stark	£2.95 pbk
_____	**The Man With The Getaway Face**	Richard Stark	£2.95 pbk

All these books are available from good bookshops, or in case of difficulty can be ordered direct from the publisher. Indicate the number of copies required and fill in the form below.

. . . .

NAME _____
(Block letters please)

ADDRESS _____

_____

Send to Allison & Busby Ltd, 6a Noel Street, London W1V 3RB. Please enclose remittance to the value of the cover price plus 50p for the first book plus 15p per copy for each additional book ordered to cover postage and packing. Applicable in the UK only.
While every effort is made to keep prices low, it is sometimes necessary to increase prices at short notice. Allison & Busby reserve the right to show on covers and charge new retail prices which may differ from those advertised in the text or elsewhere.